The
Long Road Back:
The
Death of Idealism

A Plea for Change

Dana + Bobby,

   Great seeing/speaking to you last night;
tell your mom and sisters "hello" and I
wish them my best. Looking forward to some
runs together, don't forget the defib paddles,
just incase ... Hope you enjoy my ramblings
and the book has some literary value/merit?
Love you guys; remind Bobby re my son, Colby,
if there are any openings relative to employment ... Thanks   Love, Coach P. aka

ARTHUR WHITEKNIGHT

254-9288
267-8106

outskirtspress
DENVER, COLORADO

The Long Road Back: The Death of Idealism
A Plea for Change

Outskirts Press, Inc.
http://www.outskirtspress.com

ISBN: 978-1-4787-6664-3

Outskirts Press and the "OP" logo are trademarks belonging to Outskirts Press, Inc.

PRINTED IN THE UNITED STATES OF AMERICA

Preface

This is a story which has to be related; an incident in life which must be shared with all people, especially those who have found themselves in a similar situation. Throughout my formative years (those encompassing 1-22) I was always taught that one should constantly strive towards and practice certain cherished human instrinsics- honesty, sincerity, helping others, fairness in all dealings involving ethical decisions. Sometimes, however, unfortunate circumstances may evolve to strike at and embitter those who tend to believe in the inherent nobility of the human spirit. Idealism becomes impractical, intrinsics and Utopian theory too often remain in the classroom and are constantly compromised in the overly practical, materialistic world of survival.... Nepotism, politics, and the "Who you know" approach have become the priorities, while principles and morality have been sacrificed in the name of expediency and simply getting ahead in life's little game plan.

Nowhere has the latter philosophy become more evident than in the microcosm known as public education; the "hallowed halls of ivy" concept has been infiltrated and undermined by politics which certainly shouldn't have any place or influence in our academic institutions. It's a sad and sorry commentary to accept; nevertheless, it's a reality with which the educator has been coerced to cope and adapt. This situation, however, doesn't preclude one from waging a constant struggle to overcome and expose existing abuses; hence, you have the secondary motivation for this book. You will learn the primary motivational factor in the last chapter.

To become a victim of circumstance in a very politically fabricated "frame-job" has to be a fate worse than death, and the story which is about to unfold within these pages will endeavour to present one such occurrence. God only knows the number of situations like this that may have evolved!

The following tale merits the attention of every caring and concerned individual who gives a damn about the future of education in this country.

What about the skeptics? Could the author be manipulative to the point of using "hype" in order to create controversy and $ales, to sacrifice the altruistic creation for the financial gain brought about by a successful novel? The reader will ultimately have to accept the responsibility for making that judgment call based upon his or her "gut reaction." At best, the work may have some social value, and at the worst, the blatant politics and accompanying hypocrisy present in our educational system may be exposed for the malignancy that it's become.

If you dare then, dear reader, prepare yourself for a memorable sally forth into a seemingly endless wasteland of treachery, deceit, and political decadence wherein the value and dignity of human life become expendables when they conflict with political or nepotistic considerations.

The book is dedicated to my sons (Ross and Mason), to all of my former students and athletes, and young people everywhere; to anyone who may have found him/herself in a similar dilemma; to anyone who can empathize and become more involved in making meaningful changes that might benefit teachers and students alike; and, lastly, to the power urchins who hopefully might experience a conscience-raising catharsis to atone for all of the manipulation which often feeds their shallow, empty lives.

Chapter 1:

The Warning

I had just completed my graduate work at Penn State and was wide-eyed as well as eager to attempt to apply all of that lovely theory to an actual classroom situation. My mother had phoned me on the evening of August the 20th to inform me that my dad might lose his job, and that they would greatly appreciate my returning to the area in order to help out with things in case they needed me.

At this time (the late 60s) the demand for teachers was great while the supply was rather limited; it was an extremely difficult decision to make since I had planned to pursue my studies toward a doctorate with all expenses paid. Since Don Quixote is my all-time favorite hero, however, how could I do anything else but return home to teach in one of the local high schools? After all, my parents had sacrificed for me throughout most of their lives and it seemed only proper that I might have the opportunity to return the favor.

Within a two week span I had secured five job offers to teach English and French at the secondary level; I finally accepted one at Politico High School. I would accept an additional responsibility- coaching golf. To say that my knowledge of the latter sport was limited would be a gross understatement at the very least; however, it proved, not only challenging but rewarding as well! I thought about it at great length, and accepted the position offered to me and anxiously awaited the first day....

The first impressions were positive; the kids seemed very nice, the discipline was generally good in the school, but it would become increasingly obvious that too much emphasis was being placed on certain sports. The principal (Mr. Marionette who had a goodly amount of difficulty enunciating the King's English) was himself a former jock and staunchly supported the football program. The school comprised a jointure which included three towns and I had previously graduated from one of the original, pre-jointure schools. This is how it all began....

I was cautioned by one of my former teachers that my hiring caused quite a stir since the job I had secured had evidently been promised to the son of some crony-friend of the superintendent's; however, my appointment became official at the public meeting due to a lack of communication and understanding among five board members and Mister Dowrong, the superintendent. The super was a diminutive, weasel-like man whose integrity and honesty always seemed to be in question. I had been duely warned by Miss French about the quagmire into which I had quite innocently entered. On a Wednesday I walked into the language lab; the fourth week of school had quickly sped by and Miss French and I had become good friends; she informed me that she wanted to share a bit of information which disturbed her.

"Art, did you know that you're not one of the principal's favorite people? As a matter of fact, you are number one on his shit list."

"Why Ann? To what do I attribute this great honor? My glowing personality, my teaching ability, the way I spell my last name?"

"Let's not be cute; this is quite serious. His dislike for you stems from deep political roots. It would seem that your teaching position was 'promised' to someone else. Were you aware of that fact?"

"No, however, I've had vibes that he harbored animosity toward me based upon his expressions and the manner in which he speaks to me."

"Well, to make a long story short, he will do anything within his power to make you look bad or negligent in the hope that you'll submit and resign. He and Mister Dowrong have formed an alliance and they've put out a contract on you, so to speak, I only hope that you can handle the pressure because you're due for more than your share."

"Why should he bother to harass me? How could he possibly find fault with such a wonderful guy such as myself? My ability to teach and the rapport demonstrated between teacher and student is really all that should matter."

From day one, therefore, the administration and certain members of the Board were involved in a premeditated conspiracy against yours truly (the starry-eyed idealist). My 'promised' job had to be returned to its rightful owner, after all, in the world of politics, human lives and reputations had become expendable. "Blood was thicker than water" while qualifications and ethics had no right getting in the way of an obviously correctable error. Come hell or high water, the decision had been rendered that I would have to be eliminated in some expedient manner; nothing that would arouse too much interest or controversy, however.

It became increasingly evident that I was to become intensely involved in a political chess game which was undertaken to besmirch my professional life and, more importantly, the very core of my dignity. The plans were laid, and the events that were to follow would snowball and create a living nightmare.

Within the span of the months that followed my first day of employment, I became painfully aware of how sinister, vicious and hypocritical some people can become. The principal (Mr. Marionette) became an unwitting pawn himself and was programmed to create as much aggravation as possible in my workday; all too frequent classroom observations, false accusations regarding tardiness, verbal abuse in the presence of students, questions and innuendos were circulated implying everything from drug use to affairs with students. At times words didn't suffice when attempting to convey gut feelings and this would certainly be a case in point. No one could possibly empathize with someone who's unfortunate enough to be in this type of a situation; I was experiencing the total spectrum of human emotions- everything from self-pity to the volatile and primitive urges to lash out at somebody responsible. The turmoil, the emotions, and the pressures were overwhelming and my personality began to subtley change as my faith in my fellow-man continued to wane. I felt that I was closing myself within myself; I assumed an antisocial and introverted character which tended to shut people out. My hands were tied and I understood for the first time in my life the meaning of the time-worn cliche regarding justice being blind; in other words, it was my character and my integrity pitted against their rumors and falsehoods.

Even some friends began hearing some rather demeaning things about my "sordid, perverse" lifestyle. Alice Meanwell who was a very trusted friend of the family called one night to inform me that a certain member of the Board had made an off-color remark to the effect that, on occasion, I had gone to school drunk.

"Hello Art, is that you?"

"Yes, how are you doing, Alice?"

"Great! I'm surprised that you recognized my voice; it's been too long since I've talked to you. I've been so busy now that I'm a committee woman, and I simply can't find the time to do the things I know I should do. Well, anyway, I had to let you know what was said on Monday night at the Gossip House by Clarence Patton; mind you, I was sitting there and overheard what was said. I must tell you that I really became furious when I overheard the comments made by Mr. Patton. I would have thought that he had more brains and possessed more tact than that! It seems that he had heard this from some 'reliable' source that you were not only drinking excessively but that you were also carrying on an on-going relationship with one of your students."

She was personally appalled but couldn't become involved because she feared possible reprisals from her boss who happened to be Patton's brother. She feared, therefore, that her employment and job security might prove to be short-lived. She wanted to know why he apparently had it in for me.

Chapter 2:
"The Snow Job"

The shit hit the fan prior to the Christmas break; let me expand on the latter incident.

I was called into the office by Principal Marionette who proceeded to verbally chastise me regarding a ski trip which I had chaperoned on the previous evening. I had volunteered myself to function as the advisor for the ski club; I took one bus a week to Elk Mountain and the reservations were determined on a first come, first serve basis as well as by my own personal screening based upon behavior and attitude previously demonstrated.

Arlene, one of the Board director's daughters, and Paul had come to me earlier that day to request a seat on the bus.

"I'm sorry about that, Arlene, but the bus is filled."

"Please," responded Paul, "we're looking forward to going this week and we would both be very grateful if you could help us out some way, Mr Whiteknight."

"Perhaps, if you could meet me there, I may be able to secure student rates and save you about five dollars. Better yet, there may be some complementary passes left."

"That would be great, could you?" they both agreed.

After having reached the slope, distributing the tickets,

and taking care of the rentals, Paul and Arlene showed up with four other people. Playing Mr. Nice guy, I gave each of them a reduced ticket, only after making another trip to the ticket window. They thanked me and were gone. Fancying myself Jean Claude Kiley, I couldn't wait to attack the slopes.

I've a personal philosophy on just about everything from friendship to Xanidu and skiing is no exception. You simply have to observe me ski ski in order to guess what type of mood I happen to be in at the time; feelings, frustrations, and disappointments can be therapeutically removed when attacking the mountain- even joy and happiness can be realized. By the end of the evening, therefore, no matter how bleak the day, I'm physically and, more importantly, spiritually atoned; nothing matters more than enjoying life, attempting to live it to its fullest because it's rather short to begin with and people should shrug off any negative or misdirected energies. I returned to my apartment, after waiting for the last parent to pick up their offspring, completely "mellowed out" and at peace within and without. Unfortunately, the following morning would inevitably unfold together with all of the lies and nonsense!

"Mr. Whiteknight, I received a very disturbing phone call late, very late last night from Mr. Wattage; he informed me that his daughter didn't return from the ski trip until 2 a.m. He was very upset as well as concerned about his daughter's whereabouts and he questioned her about the incident. Arlene told her father she was with you last night until that time. Well, what do you have to say for yourself?"

I had to try to maintain my composure during the implied moral assassination; however, my emotions got the best of me and I proceeded to lower myself by lashing out at my judge

and jury by bringing the following facts to light: 1. Paul and
Arlene were to tell their parents that they couldn't come on
the bus since there was no room and I, therefore, wouldn't be
responsible for them in anyway, 2. After giving them their reduced lift tickets, I hadn't seen them for the remainder of the
night until we were leaving on the bus. Since it began to snow
lightly, I asked them to follow the bus and to go home because
the roads might become quite treacherous and slick. When I
returned to the school, I waited until the last student had gone
home before I left; the time was approximately 11:25 p.m.

Paul, Arlene and the other four desperados who were in
their company had entirely different plans which were re-
vealed to me later that day during the process of my investigation relative to what had actually taken place on that fateful
night. Some of the other students informed me concerning
what had transpired; they had gotten sidetracked and had
evidently taken a wrong turn; how amazing it was that they
turned up in Narrowsburg, New York where the legal drinking age just happened to be 18, not 21 as it is in Pennsylvania.
Equally amazing was the fact that this locality was 180 degrees north of their intended destination, namely the high
school! To make a long story and contrived story short, the
other kids told me that it was their intention all along to go
drinking following the skiing. Obviously, I had been deceived
and set-up as the scapegoat…Even to this day, some 14 years
later, Mr. Wattage believes his lovely, lying daughter. I requested principal Marionette to call Paul, Arlene and their
parents into the office so that I could confront them with
the truth, but they were absent from school; evidently, the
hangover must have been too traumatic for their frail, little

bodies and equally weak minds.

Marionette refused to pursue it and the issue was dropped, after all, he didn't want to see Mr. Wattage's daughter publicly embarrassed or ridiculed by fellow students. I finally resolved to phone Arlene's parents in order to get an apology and to present them with the cold, hard facts, but attempting to reason with him was like beating one's head against the proverbial wall: "His daughter had never lied to him before so why would she start now?"

I rest my case....they refused to admit any wrongdoing or guilt in the matter. The bullshit continued and they had stooped to new lows by getting their very own kids involved; the plot began to thicken and I was concerned whether or not I would survive my first year of teaching, never mind my tenure.

Chapter 3:

God Give Me "Guidance"

I've never taken life too seriously; that's why I proceeded to lose 25 pounds over the next two months; I was hospitalized on the suspicion I might have developed a bleeding ulcer. I've always been calloused and insensitive like that- I would never allow anybody or anything to get to me!

My situation continued to metamorphosize me into a completely different human being and I became stagnated in self-pity; I resolved that I wouldn't make a good martyr and chose to redirect my emotions and energies into a more constructive channel. This decision came about none too soon, for timing became critical at this juncture of my life. My life seemed to be passing before me and I wasn't enjoying it because I was constantly being placed on the defensive; I had also slipped into a prolonged state of depression. The old cliche certainly applied in that you only go around once, so one should live every moment to its fullest as if it were your last. In an attempt to restore my faith in my fellow man, I took a charter flight to Europe with my roommate; we backpacked, bummed around and encountered some gracious, wonderful people as well as realized some super, memorable experiences. I returned refreshed and hopeful that I'd been appointed to a new position as a guidance counselor; unfortunately, things didn't work out....

When I returned from Europe, I became involved in my second year of semi-professional football (I required therapy beyond the ski slopes); I discovered that Mr. Dowrong's daughter had been appointed to the vacated guidance position which I deemed to be a travesty since I was highly qualified and she was not. As a matter of fact, she had only recently begun to pursue her master's degree, whereas, I had already earned my master's equivalency and would only have to complete my practicum while functioning on the job. Once again, I was crushed by their complete lack of integrity and professionalism, and I resolved not to allow them to get away with it this time; I intended to challenge them, even if it meant my job! I was never so thoroughly pissed off in my entire life; I, therefore decided to grieve her appointment and secure some sense of justice or so I thought...

I began my investigation into the matter by returning to the district office, where I was informed that my application had never been received or perhaps it had been misplaced somewhere. I was seeing red; what can I say? I had hand delivered the application myself before leaving for Europe and had naively included original recommendations from the Dean of Men's office where I had earned my degree. Evidently, my application had been beamed up by Scotty to the Starship Enterprise.

My immediate reaction was one of fury, intense fury that they could stoop to that level of dishonesty; that they believed they could so openly go against morality and hope to get away scot-free was truly appalling. I bolted over to Dowrong's intersanctum and aided by an adrenaline rush, accidentally tried to pull the door open when I actually should have pushed; the door knob broke off in my hand!

He was quite pompous and arrogant in his demeanor when he asked if there was any problem and, if so, could he be of service? He leered over his spectacles and asked, "Is there anything I can help you with, Mr. Whiteknight? People usually have the decency to knock before they enter this room; what's the meaning of this intrusion?"

"To answer your first question, may I offer that you've done quite enough to me already and even more to benefit your daughter; I suppose she doesn't possess any conscience either since your blatant lack of scruples may have some genetic origin. Don't talk to me of decency and social amenities because you don't have a thread of either in your entire body! What's more, Mr. Dowrong, if you weren't such a frail, old buzzard, I would probably jack you up against the wall to teach you some humility. You're nothing but a poor excuse for a human being and I'm not about to be intimidated by the likes of you- job or no job. I intend to fight you on this one."

I slammed the door, but not before launching the door knob past his head; luckily, I was in enough control so that I didn't throw it directly at him, although I've often regretted not having done so- posterity would be far better off without individuals like Mr. Dowrong. The naked ape within me had finally surfaced; at least the brass door knob was more genuine than the individual at whom it was hurled. The mind games and the war would continue… It was, however, well-worth the possible flack because the fear, the sheer terror in his eyes made everything worthwhile. I was left with a sense of catharsis as well as fulfillment.

By the way, Nell didn't receive her degree until June of 1976, some two years later. It was proudly written up by her gloating parents in the local newspapers- the "hype" involved might lead one to suspect that she had earned her doctorate or found the missing link or something of that monumental nature.

The grievance didn't go anywhere because I couldn't prove conclusively that I ever applied for the position.

Chapter 4:
"Who's the Real Thief?"

Approximately one month later, I was accused of misappropriating funds for the golfing requisition by none other than Mr. Honesty, Dowrong himself. I received word through principal Marionette that the Board requested that I be present at the next working session so that they could get to the bottom of everything; naturally, I agreed to be there. The meeting was a farce; they handled all business matters from hiring maintenance men to deciding whether or not to remove candy machines from school property; it seems that one of the Board members was adamantly opposed since they happened to be his machines; however, Mr. Jacque obviously didn't perceive the conflict of interest. I held my cool minute after minute until two hours plus had transpired. The super Dowrong was present, but when the business agenda had ended, he feigned a weak spell and quickly excused himself. The new business manager, who was a nephew of Dowrong's- let's hear it again for nepotism- was left "to mind the store'. It proved to be more like "holding the bag." I had patiently waited and listened to the pent-up charges and could scarcely believe my ears.

"Mr. Whiteknight ordered golf supplies without the administration's permission; he has proven to be most insubordinate and he persists in not following the proper channels," quoted Jim Flunky, the timid mouthpiece of the Little Prince. Of course, he read every word from a hand written sheet which was given to him by Dowrong before the latter exited.

"Mr. Whiteknight, do you have anything to say in your behalf in response to these charges?' bellowed the Board president.

Boy, did I ever; I had anticipated all of this crap and was well-prepared with documentation and a key witness to disprove the super's flimsy falsehoods. I proceeded to methodically rip apart all of the so-called accusations. There was one charge, however that I didn't forsee; it implied that I was personally responsible for an automobile accident on the way to a golf match at the end of the previous season. This was truly ironic because I had been advocating, since my first year of coaching, that the school district provide some means of transportation for the "lesser" sports. I was concerned that something tragic might occur sooner or later, and, unfortunately, it did.

We were traveling to the Poconos and it was a rather dreary day; three cars were in our convoy and I was the lead car since the other two drivers (seniors) didn't know the route to the course where we were to compete. We reached the course one-half hour early and the match went off without a hitch. One the way home, however, lightning was to strike; luckily, no one was seriously injured. We were close to the home exit and everyone went their separate way since the cars were arranged according to the towns in which the kids lived. There was a sudden torrential downpour and the last car had evidently skidded off the road and down an embankment. John called me later that night relative to what happened; immediately, I phoned the boy's parents to make certain that John as well as the other team members were alright. His mother was livid to put it mildly and she threatened to call several of the Board members- there's the irony of it all! The following day, there was a special note on the announcements which stated that school policy had always existed forbidding students from traveling to and from sporting events without provided transportation- another fabrication on their part because no such policy had ever been documented on or off the books. They had the nerve to take that unfortunate incident and attempted to manipulate it to their own advantage while they hung me out to dry once again.

With respect to the "misappropriation of funds", it wasn't possible to order any supplies without the principal's and business manager's co-signatures on a purchase order that was then given to me. I had learned my lesson well when I had applied for the guidance position and I had adopted the practice of making photostats to protect myself because there was no honor among men like this. Not only did I produce the copies, but the manager of the sporting goods store in question supported my position and testimony.

Finally, the insubordination and not going through the proper channels garbage reduced itself to my word against his; in the process I had brought to light what had transpired regarding my application for guidance counselor and that this man was obviously harbouring a serious grudge. What the hell, I was on a roll so I concluded my remarks by stating that I intended to resign as golf coach unless the Board did something relative to providing safe transportation for the athletes.

I figured that it was all over for me but the shouting in any event! Perhaps, it had something to do with the fact that we had won the school's first championship or the fact that we finished the season undefeated or that we produced five all-stars or that one of those all-stars placed 17th in the state- I really don't know to this day, however, I would hope that the truth entered into the scenario somewhere because I was very much taken back by their response…Thanks were extended to the collective Board members for listening to my version of the story; again, I had a gut-feeling that they'd probably ask me to resign my teaching position as well because they couldn't deal with the truth.

Surprisingly, six of the nine members extended their hands in apology, and I came close to experiencing a massive coronary. The battle had been waged and won but the war was far from over! I still savour that memory; the following year, super Dowrong would be forced into an early retirement, however, the intrigue and conspiracy would continue to plague my life, I suppose that this would be his legacy.

Chapter 5:
"You Can't Fight City Hall"

The following November, elections were held and some rather alarming results evolved; the directors that had been most empathetic and supportive in my time of need either resigned or were voted out by their constituents. Of course, implicit throughout was the fact that the federal law enforcement people were investigating and prosecuting board directors from surrounding districts and our school was rumored to be one of the next on their list. Plea-bargaining became the craze and one guy was ratting on another to save his own miserable skin. The individuals who were most hurt by the decadence and political corruption were the students. A beautiful Taj Mahal ($12.9 million) edifice had been constructed and quite a few pockets had been lined to the max. "Little things" in the construction were overlooked; the athletic field, for instance, lacked proper drainage and was dug up since it hard turned into a bloody quagmire.- the co$t , you ask? It turned out to be a mere pittance, a bargain to the district's taxpayers because they had to shell out an additional $35,000 simply because it wasn't done properly in the first place; it required drain tile.

Enough said about the blatant abuses, the "rip-offs"; it would be a rather easy matter to list and detail an additional

25 such "Catch 22's"; however, this is not my purpose.

Getting even became the bottom line philosophy of two vengeful Board members as well as the principal who had unwittingly became involved in the personal vendetta; the men that I had won over were no longer there and the individuals who replaced them would prove to be extremely hostile toward me. These political, bottom-dwellers were of the opinion that I should be removed; I had become a threat, too independent, too outspoken, too individualistic and too smart for my own good, whatever that meant! Marionette was always a staunch supporter of the Dowrong philosophy on life and he informed me on several occasions that I had not heard the last from him or Mr. Super. Once again events would unfold which confirmed my suspicions; factions would unite in order to create a vacancy so that my job could be surrendered to someone more "deserving and worthy". The nightmare was begun anew... the principal would contrive a plan which appeared foolproof on the surface, nevertheless, the conspirators would be frustrated once more....

Chapter 6:

"Above the Law"

I had recently completed some coursework and credits at the local university, received the transcript, and went to the district office in order to update my personal file because the Master's plus 15 column meant an increment in my salary. Upon close examination of said file. I happened to come across an interesting piece of documentation which had been inserted by super Dowrong without my knowledge or signature; this document violated the teacher union's contractual language in no uncertain terms, for no document was to be placed into a teacher's personal file unless the teacher had been given an opportunity to read, comment on and sign said document. The signature didn't necessarily signify agreement, however, the bottom line was that the document (must be signed). The only signatures that actually appeared on the combination rating scale/character analysis were those of the super and principal.

The rating scale that was utilized indicated that I was negligent in performance of my duties as a teacher/coach, had a very hostile, negative attitude; couldn't accept constructive criticism; was chronically late to class; was insubordinate to my superiors; didn't go through the proper channels in school matters etc… The vindictive character bashing continued.

Obviously, I grieved this infringement of my rights and despite being threatened by both Dowrong as well as Marionette, I refused to submit. I pursued the grievance and eventually won. Battle #3 had been waged and secured! The super was ordered to remove the derogatory material from my file and he was cautioned not to repeat the offense with anyone else.

Despite the latter incident, Marionette warned, "We haven't finished with you yet; you'll regret ever having fought us because I personally won't rest until I see you removed from the teaching and coaching profession, Whiteknight."

I couldn't grieve this because it was my word vs. his; nevertheless, my resolution and my will to win became even stronger and I vowed to myself that I would expose these asses for what they were and what they represented

Chapter 7:
"The Great Flood"

It was the summer of '72 when hurricane Agnes overflowed the banks of the mighty Susquehanna in several nearby communities; our Shop teacher (Mr. Dedicado) was the close friend of someone who owned a car dealership in one of the flooded areas. The individual phoned Sam about the possibility of transporting a few of the totaled or irrepairably damaged autos to our high school so that the students in the electronics and mechanical classes might be able to work on these automobiles. Sam was elated and grateful regarding his friend's offer/suggestion; the whole process was set into motion and Sam anxiously awaited the delivery of the damaged cars.

In the process of being granted approval to follow through on his plan, Sam had to contact Dowrong to make him aware of the intended sequence of events. Believe it or not, super Dowrong intercepted these automobiles and had them delivered to a body shop; they proceeded to strip the autos of anything useful and/or $aleable before they reached their final destination at the high school.

This sorry scenario presents an exemplary insight to the man's true character or, more appropriately, his lack of any!

Chapter 8:

"Illicit Conversation"

I recall running in the Jim Thorpe 10 kilometer race and I met a friend with whom I had previously competed in several races, including the Boston Marathon; Jerry taught and coached at a nearby school district and proved to be a valued friends and a hell of a person. He was all flustered and I could tell something was bothering him; he informed me that his commanding officer at Reserves, who also happened to be one of the new school board directors, had made statements to the effect that I was involved in drug trafficking. I personally believe that Jerry was as pissed off about the whole situation as I. Of course, he was in a rather tenuous position and couldn't get directly involved since this guy was his superior officer- deja vous, bingo, the same old tune, different singer!

"Art, where do these assholes get off thinking that they can say and do whatever they please; I know that it's nonsense. What the hell do those guys have against you?" asked Jerry.

"The answer to that question is really quite simple- they want my job for one of their own, and Dowrong is trying to get even over what has transpired thus far." I gave him a synopsis of the more salient events that had evolved.

"What the hell, Art, I run with you; we've competed

together in how many races now and I've never seen you use any drugs, not even an aspirin when you probably should have before that other 10 kilometer race; you thought that it might upset your stomach. This whole thing stinks, and I'll do what I can to help you," defiantly stated Jerry.

"Hey, Jerry, every dog has his day; I wouldn't trade places with any one of those bastards for all of the sake in Japan because when they kick-off and appear before the Pearly Gates, they'll be in for some serious shit."

"Well, anyway, what do you intend to do about this little dilemma; please don't get too bent out of shape and do something that you may regret later on… they are probably hoping that you'll go primitive and do something stupid which they could use against you. Be careful and try to think before you act!"

I pondered my alternatives and decided to call the individual who Jerry had identified- Mr. Clarence Patton. I would have much preferred an actual audience with this character, however, because I like to read a man's eyes and gestures to determine his sincerity. Since that wasn't possible, I was forced to do the next best thing, so I proceeded to use Ma Bell.

"Hello, may I speak to your father, please?"

"Yes, hello, who's this" asked Patton.

"This is Art Whiteknight and I've been informed by a reliable source that you're undertaking a very negative, vicious attack against my character with you rumors and innuendoes."

"Mr. Whiteknight, is this some kind of a joke? Whatever are you talking about?"

I knew that he wouldn't admit to having anything to do with it; however, I calculated that I might be able to leave him with a lasting impression. I soon achieved my objective…

"Mr. Patton, I know for a fact that you slandered me, so let's not play games here and continue to assert innocence in the matter. Let's not continue to waste each other's valuable time either. At the very least, be man enough to admit to your part in this ridiculous plot. Look, I'm going to caution and advise you before you spout out another meaningless utterance; choose your words more carefully from now on; if I hear that you've even implied something off-color about me, one of two options will be executed. The choices are quite simple really and here they are: 1) You can get lucky in which case I will abuse you physically (or) 2) You can get unlucky and be prosecuted to the full extent of the law for your slanderous accusations; one way or the other, you'll pay dearly for your stupidity as well as your ignorance in attempting to destroy my life. The choice is yours…"

"I swear to you, Art, I never said that; don't be so bitter and angry. We have nothing against you, believe me. Everyone on the Board feels that you're a fine teacher and you've more than proven yourself as a coach."

"What you say to my face, or rather, over the phone doesn't seem to accurately reflect what's said behind my back. I only hope that you have listened to what I've said. I'll be damned before I lie down and allow you people to dump all over me simply because I don't know the 'right people'. Stuff your lame flattery and ingenuous patronage; I don't need it!"

By the way, at the time I was running 70 miles a week in preparation for my second marathon which I ended up running in 3:19:41 (not a bad accomplishment for such a low-life drug abuser…).

Chapter 9:
"Framed and Bottomed Out"

Something strange occurred later that fall; I was actually appointed wrestling coach basically because it was a new sport and absolutely no one on the faculty of any "consequence" wanted the job. I felt like a little kid in a candy store; it was always a personal dream to be realized. I had competed in football (college and semi-pro), cross country, and skiing; however, wrestling was my first love.

Since I didn't have a family at this point in my life, wrestling was no.1 on my list of priorities; I ate, drank and slept the sport, and introducing it to the kids was quite a thrill for me. I wasn't even compensated for my time the first year, and we were forced to participate in an already established league or else go with a junior varsity schedule for the entire year; we chose to get our feet more than wet that initial year by going varsity, however, it proved to be well worth all of the adversity, all of the bumps and bruises, all of the necessary trials and tribulations that we were to experience that first year- we most definitely paid our dues! We finished that season at 4-6. The following year, however, something very interesting took place as the team began to mature because our record improved to 13-4; some of the kids were chosen to the League All-Star team, and three of the wrestlers placed third at the District meet to qualify for Northeast Regionals in only their second year of competition. We began to realize these honors and we were drawing significant crowds in a relatively short period of time. Everything was ahead of plan and, more importantly, life was once again becoming enjoyable as well as fulfilling...

Reflecting back conjures up a collection of fond, but dusty memories. Since the school in which I taught was located in an area which seemed to be dominated by football, basketball, and baseball; wrestling seemed a rather alien and somewhat strange sport. I hadn't been exposed to the sport myself until I was a junior in college following football season. It was a rather novel and amusing scenario in which I met the school's first coach, a man by the name of John Hoppy. He had situated himself immediately outside the shower room area; there he stood (he was a munchkin) with his no.2 pencil and clipboard gawking at some of the guys in the shower, including moi.

Gay Right proponents as of yet hadn't come out of the closet, nor was the issue of homosexuality a very popular topic of discussion; nevertheless, we all shared some considerable doubts/misgivings when we saw this little dude "checking out the masses of asses", the collective stockpile of studs that were assembled there within. As we exited the showers, coach Hoppy asked if my name was Whiteknight to which I responded a timid "yes". He glanced down at his clipboard and scribed a check next to what appeared to be my John Hancock.

"Art, do you think you might be interested in trying something a little more challenging than football? My name's

John Hoppy and I've been hired to coach the university's first wrestling team."

"Please, how could any sport be as tough and challenging as football? What do you mean by wrestling any way? That stuff on television, the WWF or whatever they call it?"

"No, not exactly, collegiate, folkstyle wrestling which is considerably different from the so-called professional nonsense."

"Coach, I honestly don't know at this point because my work schedule and hours are rather inflexible and I have some really tough coursework this semester."

"I understand, but you can't blame a guy for trying; I watched some of your buddies and you working out in the weight room and I have to say I was pretty impressed by your work ethic; I personally believe that you would make an excellent wrestler and I'm attempting to get some semblance of a team together this year so that we might get a little bit of a head start on next year's season. If there's any chance at all that you can make it tomorrow at 6 o'clock, come to the wrestling room- you won't regret it!

I'll have to admit that I was more than a little curious and to make a long story, short, I attended the practice session on the following day and got duely bitten by the bug. I loved all sports (especially football) and I believed in what Plato was espousing in The Republic regarding the importance of balancing the activities of the body with those of the mind- it made a great deal of sense to me… but this wrestling was unbelievably challenging and significantly tougher in every sense of the word!

The more that I learned, the more I grew in respect and admiration of the sport, despite the fact that I was getting my hard ass kicked all over the wrestling room by teammates and a certain coach who was only half my size and strength. Coach Hoppy held an intramural tournament after about a month of instruction and to my surprise I was fortunate enough to take first place in my weight class. It taxed me physically, mentally and spiritually and, in a sense, changed my life and character for the better.

Walking off the mat a winner or champion left me with a feeling that is difficult to share or express because it has to be experienced first hand; it can't be a vicarious thing! Winning three consecutive semi-pro football championships was both awesome and monumental but wrestling takes one to a higher level of intensity, concentration, sacrifice and dedication. When you're out there, there's no place to run or hide, there aren't any teammates picking you up when you sink into deplorable states of depression or covering your mistakes- errors usually end in defeat. There's only you and your opponent, your body, mind and spirit; and, yes, the inescapable presence of the clock, ticking off 6 to 7 minutes that will test you to your limits and often beyond!

I've grown to love that feeling, that natural high, that intensity!!! Even marathons left me with a great sense of achievement and exhilerating rushes of adrenaline, but nothing comparable to competitive wrestling...

I learned a great deal about myself as well as others through this sport. During my final year at the university, I recall competing against a blind wrestler from Franklin and Marshall University; to understate the situation, my emotions were quite mixed. Was he supposed to be physically challenged or was he considered to be handicapped? I was experiencing great difficulty in getting "pumped-up" for the match. Coach Hoppy gave me what turned out to be the best advice possible at the time; unfortunately, I heard what he had to say but I didn't listen!

"Art, he's one of their best wrestlers; that may be hard to believe but you had better listen to what I'm telling you! He's very tough, especially on the top and bottom, and you'll have to maintain hand contact on your feet so that he'll always know exactly where you are on the mat. If you make the mistake of feeling sorry for this guy, he'll pin your ass. Go out and be aggressive like you always are; treat him as you would any other opponent."

Guess what? I learned, first hand, the true meaning of humility, sensitivity, pride and the dignity of the human spirit-the bugger beat me 4-3! What a humbling lesson that would prove to be because I had really given it my best shot; I ended up feeling more respect and admiration for Rob following the match than disappointment in/for myself... Coach Hoppy was right on the money in his advice and that experience will forever remain etched in my memory.

I attempted to develop my ability in the sport and continued wrestling, beyond my senior year at the university, but also while attending graduate school. I've attended too many clinics to remember and I've competed in numerous tournaments; more importantly, I've witnessed what the sport can do for kids who lack discipline or direction in their lives, and the results have been far more positive than negative... and thank God for that.

I imagined it was obvious to my enemies that the sport was a very important part of my life, and Achilles heel, if you will.

Therefore, what better way to get even, than by taking away the coaching job? This is my personal theory based on a careful analysis of the events that would follow. They were confident that they had zeroed in on my primary weakness which would eventually break my spirit to fight back, my will to win. To add injury to insult and to solidify their argument that I was a misanthrope, principal Marionette "brow beat" four of my fellow teachers into jotting down some negative comments and anecdotes in which I was once again projected as being incompetent, unprofessional, or alienated from my peers. This documentation, however, would prove to be not only sensationalized but fictionalized as well.

"If I wasn't there for the weigh-ins, Mr. Whiteknight and the wrestling team would have had to forfeit the match", asserted Ed Wizard.

This accusation was totally unfounded because I arrived 25 minutes prior to the scheduled weigh-in. There never would have been a forfeit. By the way, this misguided individual never apologized, but I still feel sorry for him because he went on to accept a head coaching job at another high school; he was supposed to rebuild their football program and he ended up being asked to resign due to his miserable failure. I suppose he did this to remain in the good graces of the administration.

Mr. Coercia contributed the following insight to further enhance my image and cause: "The showers are never turned off, things are disappearing when the wrestlers are around, someone's urinating in the basketball players lockers" (it turned out to be one of their own by the way). Any time something went wrong in the locker room area, therefore, the lads usually got blamed. The kids were being unfairly stereotyped as thieves and trouble-makers; of course, I could resign to benefit the program but that's exactly what they wanted me to do. I refused to be spat upon again and projected as the "heavy" who was most responsible for these problems. The frustration and personal aggravation increased in proportion to the lies and fabricated stories; I couldn't simply shake off the abuse, Bingo! Deja vu- to be honest about it, I couldn't hack it any more. I began feeling self-pity and even a degree of self-doubt. I had often wondered how Marionette would have felt if either he or his own son were treated in this manner?

Marionette even had the athletic director, Mr. Chaos, searching high and low for dirt that might be used against me by conducting clandestine interviews with a number of my wrestlers. He was grilling them relative to my behavior, character, and language at practice: "Is your coach using any profanities at practice? Does he knock anyone around; is he on the bus with you when you wrestle away?"

Jim Brown (the team captain) later confided that he had suggested to the A.D. that he should question me face-to-face, and stop involving the wrestlers in attempting to present coach in a bad light!

I had completed my second year of coaching wrestling (it was March of 1975). I received a note from the principal which indicated that he wanted to meet with me regarding the wrestling team; I had hoped that it might involve something of a positive nature since three of the wrestlers had placed at Districts and qualified for Regionals- wrong again… On the contrary, he proceeded to verbally condemn me regarding the team's poor conduct at two of our seventeen duals. Letters had supposedly been received from two of the schools we had wrestled earlier that season inform-ing Marionette that our team had displayed unsportsmanlike conduct during and following the meets, and had destroyed school property in the locker room areas- charges lodged almost two months following the actual competitions. I rea-soned with him that if this were true, why weren't we penal-ized for unsportsmanlike conduct during the match itself, and I wanted to know precisely what was destroyed. He re-sponded in vagueness and generalities at best and everything proved to be circumstantial. Since I was the only coach and responsible for approximately thirty wrestlers, there very possibly could have been damage done before I reached the lockers following the match.

Then came the straw that broke the camel's back; he fi-nally stated, "As of that moment I was to be suspended and relieved of all my duties relative to coaching, including golf. The administrators from the schools in question would re-fuse to compete against our school unless I were dismissed as coach." Something was obviously rotten in Denmark and I resolved to get to the bottom of it. There were simply too many "convenient" coincidences that were taking place with overly consistent regularity. The bus dispatcher had suddenly received complaints about the poor supervision on the part of the coach from one driver in particular. The list of pent up charges could go on ad infinitum but it's not worth the time, nor the space.

Marionette demanded, at this point, a response to these charges; I attempted to regain my composure. I didn't want to do anything foolish. It was so blatantly obvious that this was all a preconceived "frame-job." They were finally confident that they had me by the balls, and that there was no way out short of resignation.

One of the greatest feelings in the world was realizing that you have accomplished something that other people deemed impossible; it's sometimes termed overcoming the odds. I was between the devil and the deep, blue sea; where to turn, what to do in this dilemma? With all of the reserve I could muster, I looked my accuser in the eye and told him that he wasn't going to get away with what he was attempting to do, and that I would fight him tooth and nail; in short, I would once again file a grievance in order to regain not only my coaching positions, but, more importantly, my integrity.

"If you do that and this thing gets to arbitration, you won't be teaching here next year." I surmised that irrespective of the grievance, I wouldn't be teaching there anyway since he would contrive some other excuse for eliminating my position- and he did!

At this time I would like to dispel a possible misconception that may be surfacing "between the lines"; I certainly don't fancy myself God's gift to humanity nor do I perceive myself as a martyr; however, neither am I the incompetent, immoral bastard that the administration and some Board members were trying to project to the public through their underhanded dealings.

Despite his threat, I possessed a conscience and there was no way that I could live with myself if I at least didn't try to fight the system in the hope that the malignancy might be brought into remission. There would be no hesitation on my part; I had to continue living with the person who stared at me everyday from the other side of the mirror; I refused to heed the advice of my friends as well as my parents who suggested that I shouldn't fight them because "you can't beat politics." They all felt my job was all that should really matter, however, I felt differently.

"Mr. Marionette, when are you and your toads going to start respecting people and arrive to the realization that you can't 'dump' on fellow human beings and expect to get away with it? You're the ones who haven't learned; none of you intimidate me in the least. Stuff your bloody threats and this job, if it should come to that!"

The day following my confrontation with Marionette proved to be quite disappointing as well as depressing; Ms. Castoff (the assistant principal) took me aside in order to "bare her soul" regarding her involvement with respect to one of the letters. She apologized for the fact that she couldn't do anything to help my situation; still, she wanted me to know that Marionette had pressured her to contact her nephew (Jack Trader, principal) at one of the schools which had supposedly sent the negative correspondence; therefore, the letter wasn't mailed out of concern in an honest and ethical manner, rather it had been solicited and contrived! Ms. Castoff had only one year remaining before her deserved retirement and I knew that Marionette had coerced her in some way to contact her nephew. SHe had always been fair in every respect and because she was overly maternalistic toward me, she would often advise and counsel me (she liked to refer to me as the "free spirit") about what I might do to allay some of my greatest critics in order to get them on my side. She meant well, but I felt betrayed and hurt nonetheless.

"Art, did you know the assistant principal at Dover is my

nephew? Mr. Marionette forced me to call him about you since your team wrestled there a couple of months ago; I feel terrible about my role in this dirty business and I felt that I couldn't hold it in any longer. I only hope and pray to God that you can understand my side of it; you know that I'm retiring this spring and Marionette hinted that the Board might not accept my resignation, if I failed to cooperate. Please forgive me for what I've done to you, but I didn't have much choice in the matter."

"I feel sorry for you, Ms. Castoff; you've always been supportive and kind to me, but please don't worry about it because the situation that's evolved would have come about anyway; you and I share a common bond, in that we are both pawns in their devious games and we've both been sacrificed." Once more their vileness reared its ugly head.

My counter-attack to gain retribution and vindication was envisioned one evening while I was contemplating my options together with my next course of action. I decided that I would have to attend the Board's next public meeting in order to communicate to the people in attendance the vindictiveness and the hypocrisy of these few individuals who the public had entrusted to oversee the education of their children.

I felt that I was in a no win situation; what the hell, I was even "black-balled" by the head football coach! From day one the relationship between the football coach and yours truly had been strained at best. What aggravated me most about coach Stats had everything to do with the fact that he was the kingpin among so-called "Golden Boys." He was quite knowledgeable about football, and had experienced consider-able success; however, over the span of years as encounters between us increased, it became increasingly obvious that Stats possessed a tremendous amount of power and control. For instance, despite the jointure's three multimillion dollar buildings, we were the only public institution in the area that didn't also possess our own practice facility or feeder program for wrestling. There existed, however, a storage area/weight room combination; if the wall were taken down and school supplies moved to another location (my assistant Andy and I offered to do this at no expense to the district) the dimensions of the room would have been close to ideal. First we were told we could have the room, but shortly thereafter, the super and the principal reneged by stating that the maintenance supervisor had no place in which to relocate the school supplies. Both Andy and I recognized this lame excuse as pure, unadulterated cowpie! We were so encouraged as well as elated and then the change of heart sent us crashing back to reality!

The following year the conditioning program which was basically weight training for football was given the room in its entirety while, miracle of miracles, the damn wall and all of the school supplies as well had vanished- all at the district's expense. Needless to say, my assistant and I were gravely disappointed and more than a little pissed...

I always believed that if any two sports could complement one another, it would have to be wrestling and football; when you consider things like mental toughness, balance, explosiveness, strength gain, leverage, quickness, etc... The relationship between the two became obvious. Nevertheless, coach Stats had a few of his assistants spouting out some pretty empty falsehoods and insidious remarks with respect to wrestling. Assistants like Pat Yessman were making outrageous statements to the effect that wrestling could weaken joints by overstretching the muscles; they would have to lose huge amounts of weight and this would leave them susceptible to serious injuries; they would never be able to regain their strength once they lost weight; and, if they were desirous of playing on the varsity level the following year, they were to lift with the conditioning program to gain weight and bulk. Circulars were even distributed in which the kids with the best attendance and greatest weight and/or strength gains were proportionally praised.

Every football player (they were few and far between) who wrestled became a better athlete overall and a greatly improved football player in particular.

Whatever, in any event, it was only a matter of time before Stats and I got involved in some heated exchanges; most of the time, he would normally start off by denying everything. I can recall attempting to be somewhat diplomatic about the whole thing, but that didn't work at all. What really frosts my ass, even to this day, is the fact that he never realized how much more wrestling would have benefited his own program!

The varsity baseball coach was a personal friend and he, Larry Cecari, had complimented what wrestling had done for one of his infielders; since Ray was so small, the sports reporter was curious about where he had summoned the power to be hitting home runs. Larry responded that he had only one possible explanation; Ray had competed in wrestling and had increased his upper body size and strength tremendously. Simply for giving credit, where credit was most certainly due, Larry confided that Stats questioned him regarding the pat on the back. Additionally, he told me that Stats wouldn't talk to him for a period of about a month following the appearance of the article in the newspaper.

I'm sharing these anecdotes with you because I needed help desperately in the form of peers rallying to my support; however, here was another individual who jumped on the conspiracy band wagon because he deemed it as a good tactical move in an effort to avoid future competition for "his" athletes.

Coach Stats was also one of the resident guidance counselors. I had always believed that guidance people were there not only to administer aptitude, I.Q., and skills testing batteries but, more importantly, to stimulate or provide some encouragement and empathy to kids who may be struggling to find themselves, especially those who came from problematic homes. Sometimes they need someone to talk with; someone who may give a damn and may show a grain of sensitivity regarding whatever the problem might be. Additionally, a good counselor can often present options of which the student is unaware; for instance, here's a similar university you can consider that's more concerned with a good writing profile and grades than they are with S.A.T.'s. Stats didn't seem to share this philosophy; he was always too concerned with winning and drawing X's and O's for football team members and politicking when he could have been counseling, but these were things which comprised his priorities.

Chapter 10:
"Sensitivity Training"

The following incident occurred at the beginning of March. Stats had approached me about one of my wrestlers who also had played football for him and had helped him to secure a championship that fall. Stats informed me that I was wasting my time on Tom Davis and that it would be best to give up entirely on attempting to get him accepted to any college.

"His grades and S.A.T.'s were horrible; he was in and out of juvenile court because he had beaten up his mother's abusive boyfriend, and according to Stats, the kid was a born loser anyway, so, why even bother?"

How could a man who was responsible for helping young people be so completely negative toward a kid who was so desperately in need of help and direction, a kid who was striving to overcome a very unstable home environment, poor study habits and a violent, volatile temper? Wrestling, in my opinion, had changed Tom around 180 degrees; he was in the process of learning what self-discipline involved for the first time in his life and why it was so necessary. He excelled at the sport without ever having the benefit of a good junior high base, since he didn't participate until his sophomore year. He gave so much of himself to me that there was no way that I was going to give up on Tom; I, therefore, decided to "can" Coach Stat's advice. To be concise, Tom was accepted into college because of his wrestling potential and his academic improvement over the last two quarters. He graduated and became a very caring and productive young man. The latter story has been repeated many times since then- thank God! If it weren't for the very positive outlet that sports provide and kids like Tom, I probably would have thrown in the proverbial towel long ago, but I wasn't and never will be a quitter. I've always felt that if I could make a difference in somebody's life, then the long hours and the hard work would have been worth all of the hassles...

Chapter 11:

"The Final Confrontation Revisited"

Since I had committed myself to ignoring Marionette's threats and to pursuing the grievances, on the evening of March 12 I tried to inobtrusively seat myself in the public gallery and patiently awaited the Board's termination of all matters pertaining to business. When the moment of truth arrived for the public to share concerns and express opinions, I raised my hand to be recognized but I was avoided time after time. There were approximately 150 people present who were very much aware of what was going on and they had rallied to my support by demanding that I be allowed to address the collective board. There were even Board members who were empathetic toward my situation, unfortunately, they were in the minority and really couldn't do very much to reverse what had already transpired. To my amazement letters (voluntarily submitted) were presented supporting my abilities as a coach and my qualities with respect to my character; there were also similar commendations from fellow teachers, coaches (golf and wrestling), and a petition signed by about 500 people which clearly refuted the image that they had to sell to the public.

"He's no role-model as he would like you good people to believe; you're all wasting your time being involved with him. We've received letters attesting to the fact that Mr. Whiteknight has been remiss in his coaching responsibilities", bellowed the President of the Board. The Board solicitor, Joe Lawless, at that point cautioned Wattage about choosing his words more carefully.

"This is a democracy; we demand to hear his side of the story; let him speak", Mrs. Nicholas returned.

There was a hastily-held conference as I approached the microphone at the front portion of the auditorium.

"Very well, Mr. Whiteknight, you may speak, but we must warn you not to try to incite these people any further."

"I wasn't aware that I had incited them in the first place", I thought to myself on approaching the podium. What an ass that guy proved to be considering what he had just finished saying about me! I was tempted for a brief moment (which seemed like an eternity) to leap up on the stage and rearrange his anatomy, but I realized that it was Wattage who was attempting to infuriate me. I caught hold of my emotions after a piercing stare in his direction and proceeded to take advantage of the opportunity afforded to me.

"Ladies and gentlemen, I would like to begin by thanking you for your moral support and for the opportunity I've had in coaching some of your sons. I never expected this kind of a reaction to my dilemma; it's nice to know that somebody gives a damn. I'm certain that most people here are familiar with the fairy tale, "The Emperor's Clothes", and its moral; adults will often deceive or distort the truth in order to gain some advantage, whereas a child won't- invariably, they tell the plain, cold truth, no matter what the consequences may be."

"May I remind Mr. Whiteknight that we don't have all night!" interrupted Wattage.

"I feel that coaching is an extension of the classroom, therefore, if I'm an inept coach, I must also be an incompetent teacher. I take issue with some of the Board members as well as with principal Marionette and superintendent Dowrong, all of whom are in the process of attacking my character and integrity in the name of political expediency- there are people who want my coaching and teaching jobs. Irregardless of what you or I may do or say, it will most definitely fall on deaf ears. The letters and the petition will probably disappear or be misplaced like my application for another position once was, and nothing will be resolved here tonight, still I appreciate the encouragement."

"Mr. Whiteknight, would you kindly get to the point; we don't intend to listen to you all night!' Wattage repeated.

"I have the floor now, Mr. Wattage, and I'd thank you not to interrupt me again with your arrogant reminders. The point is this, I'm not intimidated by any of you characters and I intend to fully exercise my rights as a member of the teacher's union and, more importantly, as a man who is the complete opposite of the unsavoury character that you've endeavoured to portray. You will eventually apologize for the indignities, the injustices and that character assassination which you have inflicted upon me. My job was recently threatened if I were to pursue the arbitration procedure; well, you'd better activate that threat because I'll most definitely see you on the opposite side of the table. Not only will I clear my name, but I also intend to do my best to expose you people for the hypocrites that you are. Good night and thanks again to everyone who has tried to help- you've made my situation more bearable."

I believe that I left Wattage and the others speechless; they had probably never encountered anyone like me before and had no clue regarding what I might do next…

Chapter 12:

"Philosophical Meanderings"

The philosophy which I applied to coaching communicated to my charges that winning would come about through dedication, sacrifice and hard work. There were no substitutes for these intrinsics because sports should, in a sense, be a reflection of life; also, the greater the responsibility accepted by the kids, the greater the measure of their maturity. At this point in my life, I've encountered and have been associated with coaches who stressed winning above everything else and who used, exploited, and manipulated kids to further enhance their own self-image and/or achievements. One of my former coaches was inclined to this particular abusive approach and it often had the net result of turning my stomach. I tried to demonstrate to the kids, therefore, that along with the sweat and tears, there would also be a great deal of joy and fulfillment; it seemed important to stress the fact that there was a lot more to wrestling, golf and life than sweat and toil. The harder one worked to realize a personal goal or dream, the more one appreciated and learned to savour life because it becomes infinitely more meaningful. The Beatles (I'm an old Beatles freak from way back) said it better than anyone ever did… "and in the end, the love you take is equal to the love you make…" Whatever you put into something, you will be repaid 100% plus. These are the thoughts of the resident rebel, the drug dealer, the immoral and decadent A.C. Whiteknight…

I was correct in my assumption that the evening's events wouldn't dissuade those "righteous" men from their God-given mission. On the evening of the next public gathering, my removal became priority no.1 on their agenda and I was "kissed off" before you could blink. In my vacated spot, they appointed a "team player", a rather vacant and unscrupulous individual who had always desired one of my coaching jobs and whose father was a pillar in the community (he knew all of the influential people and was considered one himself). Stew Stabeck hoped that I'd understand they they had, more or less, forced him into taking the wrestling position; otherwise, the program might be phased out. I was naturally quite bitter, however, I gave him the team statistics from the first two seasons and wished the kids the best of luck.

He never really thanked me and he "closed" practice to all 'outsiders'; obviously, he wanted to keep me away because he was as insecure as he was inept. I would have gladly helped the kids out any way I could in order to help them attain their personal goals. If he were wise, he could have "used" me for his own benefit at practice but, of course, he didn't. Quite a few of the boys came to me about one week following the start of practice during the first week of December to express their concerns, to let me know that most of them hadn't forgotten me, and to seek my technical help.

"Coach, we can't hack it any more with that guy; practice is a joke because everybody's doing his own thing; all that he does is stands there and blows the whistle."

"He probably won't even try to wrestle with us anymore because Jeff James showed him the lights yesterday during the round-robins. The guy's a nerd and doesn't care anything about the sport; all that he seems to care about is himself. He's always mocking-out what you taught us and he's cutting you down to some of the other kids on the team; we're afraid he'll bench us if we say anything against him. Could you please do something to help us out because we're thinking about hanging it up!"

I told them to never consider quitting after all of the work they had put in during the previous year; I also asked them to refrain from criticizing him in my presence because I didn't want the kids to follow his example. In my heart I must admit that I was very pleased that his true character had surfaced since they had read through him quite well. I was concerned about what was going on; all of the hard work and effort would probably end up being flushed down the can, and the great progress made over the previous two years would probably be negated. I was angered, but what could I actually do; my hands were tied in a sense. Finally, I decided to launch a two-pronged attack. I would speak with Stabeck and confront him with his classless remarks in order to embarrass him into some type of response, and I offered to meet the kids who wanted my help at the local university's wrestling room twice a week during the evening so that it wouldn't interfere with their regularly scheduled practice. I didn't want to give Stabeck any excuses for reprimanding these wrestlers; therefore, we tried to keep it quiet.

The anticipated encounter came rather unexpectedly one

night while attending a clinic at a nearby high school. Stew seemed very nervous and attempted to steer clear of me during the first presentation; during the break, however, I took it upon myself to approach and to question him regarding his alleged off-color comments. He couldn't maintain eye contact but proceeded to deny ever having uttered the remarks- I knew that he wasn't being honest!

"Perhaps you didn't make these comments, and, then again, perhaps you did. In any event, I won't lower myself to do the same thing to you; I feel sorry for you as I do for certain other people as well because you've been manipulated and played like a fine tune but you're too naive to see it."

"What are you talking about, Art?"

"Forget it, Stew, just keep your wise-ass remarks to yourself; if you continue your present path, there's going to be trouble and bad feelings between us. Do you understand what I'm trying to say? I've tried to handle a bad situation in good faith and to give you the benefit of the doubt; I've even given you the stats for the past two season, haven't I?"

"Yes, but...."

"But nothing, that's the last time I'll speak to you about the whole mess; simply do your coaching and keep your mouth shut and there shouldn't be any trouble. Anything you have to say about me, at least be a man and have the common decency to say it to my face which is basically what I've done here."

Their season ended on a rather dismal note; the team finished the campaign at 8-7, and probably should have done much better since only three seniors had graduated from the previous year's team which had posted a 13-4 record. Three wrestlers did place at Districts and qualified for Regionals again, but they had accomplished this same feat the previous season. I was hoping that with time my bitterness would transform itself into some degree of objectivity and a renewed hope…

Chapter 13:

"An Early Christmas Present"

It was X-Mas eve of '76 and I was busy being forlorn and quite depressed reflecting on what had evolved to that point; I had lost my two coaching jobs (both of which were highly motivational factors in my life); I was denied a guidance position that most definitely should have been mine because my application had been purposely misplaced or, more likely, destroyed; and, to make matters worse (if that were remotely possible) my teaching job was on the line simply because I chose to fight the "system" by filing grievances in order to regain my coaching positions and, thereby, expose the obvious corruption. My dignity and my self-respect demanded that these people be dealt with accordingly and that I must follow through to the bitter conclusion, no matter what scenario might unfold! I knew that there would be no looking back; if I had chosen to look for another job and said to hell with this b.s., I would undoubtedly be much wealthier nowadays; however, they had backed me into a corner and attempted to assassinate my character. Therefore, I had no choice whatsoever; it was the principle of the thing and this was war...

Suddenly, there came a "rapping, a gentle tapping at my chamber door" (actually it was my front door to be exact) and upon opening it, who should appear on the threshold but one young lad named Jeffrey James bearing a gift intended for yours truly.

"Come on in, Jeff; why the gift? It's not really necessary, you know."

"Coach, most of the guys on the team thought that you deserved a lot more out of life than what you're getting now. We want you to have this as a token of our loyalty and appreciation for everything you've done for us; we also want you to know that we miss you very much and we want you back more than you'll ever know. This new guy just doesn't hack it!"

Jeff left and when I unwrapped the package, words could never do justice to the feelings that welled-up within after reading the inscription on the plaque. Needless to say, it was a very poignant moment in my life; I can think of only two other situations or experiences later on, years later that could surpass this one.

Chapter 14:
"The Arbitration Awards"

Spring was fast approaching and it hardly seemed possible; the moment of truth (the turning point in my life) was staring me in the face, for the grievances had reached the final stage. Names were struck by both sides, the battle lines were clearly drawn, the arbitrator had been selected and a date was granted for the respective arbitrations. They would be handled separately since the union advisor felt confident that this procedure would be more than advantageous to our cause. The stage was set, the players readied and the tenseness of the moment was almost unbearable. After all, not only my character but my entire future as well weighed in the delicate balance.

The following day at lunch one of my peers who had been coerced into submitting some really lame documentation against me stated, "Whiteknight would seem to be up to the proverbial creek without a paddle; man, I wouldn't want to be in his shoes for all of the money in the world", Wizard blurted in the presence of A.F. Bullet, the union president, who also happened to be a good friend. Just for the record, this character, Mr. Wizard, possessed many tragic flaws, the greatest of which was his ignorance; he chose to constantly express himself through cliches, and I actually believe that he never had an original thought in his life.

The arbitration involving golf was completed rather quickly, but a goodly amount of hostility surfaced- mainly from their side- as time after time, the conspirators projected themselves as the truly stellar people that they happened to be by contradicting their testimony (not once but several times) and ended up with their collective feet in their abusive mouths. They got caught in their lies, their fabrications, and their painfully revealing contradictions. It was so deliciously and appropriately deserved. Yes, God, there is some justice in life...

In the process of the wrestling arbitration which ensued, many other contradictions and falsified dates became blatantly apparent. For example, they had submitted the letters from the other school districts on the grounds that these letters had been voluntarily composed and mailed at the time of the actual occurrences of the indicated incidents/charges; they were supposedly, therefore, not solicited by Marionette or anyone else for that matter prior to the arbitration proceedings. However, during the cross-examination, Marionette as well as Board solicitor Guido Parodi stumbled and baulked; in the heat of battle, they had succeeded in contradicting what they had averred previously regarding the authenticity of the letters. It became quite obvious to everyone there that the letters were most definitely solicited; the one that Ms. Castoff had requested from her nephew was exposed, and the other one was mistakenly postmarked a full two months following the incident. The envelope was dated March 28 while the letter itself was dated two days following the dual meet or January 24. The stupid bastards had forgotten to falsify the postmark date on the envelope. There went their credibility and I loved it!

Every time they'd submit evidence of one kind or another, we'd refute it by countering with something more relevant or viable. For instance, the letters that were pressured from a few of my peers were ripped to shreds because we countered with letters of commendation from parents, peers, fellow coaches, and even included a letter from the league president attesting to my ability, my responsibility and, more importantly, my integrity.

The arbitration was very intense and highly emotional; it lasted for what seemed to be an eternity; it actually terminated at around the twelve hour mark. My nerves and composure proved to be far superior to Marionette's and solicitor Parodi's; I had nothing to hide while they were continually subjecting the proceedings to emotional outbursts and requested at least three recesses in order to try to regain some measure of demeanor, and to discuss their next tactical thrust. I'm not trying to be too self-righteous by saying this, but God was with me. I was morally and ethically sound and they were lying through their teeth. As with the previous encounter with super Dowrong, I savoured every moment and I never felt pressured or skeptical in any way. Following are the highlights of both arbitrations, although the wrestling award was more meaningful and personally rewarding.

Both arbitration awards overlapped in several areas; I was to be reimbursed for the season I was denied coaching by the Board since the arbitrator ruled, "that the school district had failed in both instances to justify or substantiate the actions taken and that I had been unjustly removed from and denied the positions. I was clearly the most qualified candidate as well as the most experienced applicant in the house." I was also to be reinstated for the following season. Needless to say, I was overjoyed and grateful to our union rep and our own union president, A.F. Buffett, both of whom were instrumental in saving me from the wolves; and, to my fellow "professionals" who rallied behind the cause of the opposition by submitting their own brand of smut, I hardily offer stick the "he didn't have a leg to stand on" shit up your collective *#&@%.

Yes, there was hope for the world, and, yes, one individual could, and what's more did, overcome insurmountable odds to make a difference. A precedent had been set and this would force them to think twice before attempting to destroy anyone else's character or life again. The "you can't beat city hall" philosophy had proven to be an empty cliche; my spirit soared and my faith in mankind was somewhat restored. I was convinced that the last battle had been fought and the war finally won. I felt like an Olympian marathoner, who before claiming gold, is given homage by running 400 oval with the flag of his country raised high while receiving the applause from the spectators present.

The glory and gratification of the moment would prove to be only transitory at best and the events that followed would cast me into an ever-deepening state of depression, a depression which caused me a great deal of stress and resulted in emotional scars that will remain with me for the duration of my life. This was the period of calm before the storm. I completed the final four and a half months of classes without a hitch, and I was really looking forward to the following fall when I would once again claim the job that I loved which had been unjustly denied to me.

I had received a strange phone call from Matt Niblette who

had replaced me as golf coach; he attempted to rationalize his decision for taking the job offered to him, and he had hoped that I would understand and respect his decision and that he didn't think that it should have adversely affected our friendship. Of course, if he were truly a friend, he wouldn't have accepted the "bone" that was dangled in front of him. Being the proverbial good samaritan, I decided to be as congenial as possible and told him that everything had worked out for the best and I had wished him luck. He would certainly need some because we had just reeled off two consecutive undefeated seasons in which we were the overall champions. I chose not to tell him anything regarding the arbitration award since I already decided not to reclaim that position. I also provided him with all of the stats for the kids who were returning to the team. I told him that I would try to make the transition as smooth as possible... and that was that! After all, it was in the kid's best interest anyway... at least Matt tried to make amends for his folly; the poor excuse who replaced me in the wrestling position was totally vacant of the slightest trace of integrity. Stew Stabeck was so insensitive and intellectually deficient, that he didn't even have a clue that they were manipulating him. A fellow coach who was present at the next athletic meeting (following the news regarding my arbitration award) related that Stew had given an ""Oscar-winning" performance to the Board members present; he had actually broken down and openly wept that he regretted having to step down, that he would miss the kids (most of whom didn't care for or respect him by any stretch of the imagination), and he finally thanked the Board for all of their help and cooperation in enabling him to obtain the job.

I came close to rearranging sweet Stew's anatomy one night; we both happened to be at the same night spot on this particular occasion and he was quite "wiped-out" and had inadvertently bumped into me; for that instant, I wanted to destroy him more than anything in the world. The violence abated and I regained my composure by realizing that it wouldn't be worth it- he probably wouldn't have even fought back. He was a phony and a wimp, and he lacked qualities which enabled him to function very well in their superficial world.

Chapter 15:

"The Tragedy Continues"

Once again, politics came to the forefront and the goddamned hypocrites proved themselves unscrupulous, deceitful and totally unprincipled. What they had devised, however, was truly resourceful and rather clever; I thought it to be far beyond their collective creativity, but, nonetheless, I believe in giving them some degree of credit.

Everything was going fine; I was working construction that summer in order to earn some extra money for whatever eventuality; I was in the process of purchasing some real estate on which to construct the house that I had designed. After busting my hump all day, I arrived home (I was living with my parents) at about 4:30. I sat down to collect my thoughts and to read the paper when what to my wandering eyes should appear but an article detailing the proceedings at the most recent school board meeting.

"Due to a decrease in student enrollment, the Politico School District would be forced to lay off some of its teaching staff in the elementary, science, and language subject areas."

In the final analysis, however, I was the only teacher to actually be "furloughed." Marionette's words came back to "haunt" me; I could recall them so clearly, "If you intend to continue these coaching grievances you may also end up without a teaching job."

At this point (the all-time low of lows) I recall reflecting that I very much regretted returning to the area in order to pursue my teaching career; in the final analysis, I should have remained at P.S.U. to earn my doctorate, but I had to help out at home if my parents needed me.

The manner in which they informed me that I was being "let go" showed a lot of class on their part, but, then, that was to be expected, I suppose. I read about it in the paper and three days later, I received a registered letter from the district office- quite tacky, bordering on crude I thought!

That week I again regressed into a self-pity trip with all of the trimmings; too much partying, getting violent, asking why me over and over, cheap/superficial relationships with the opposite sex because I didn't want anyone getting too close. I had a deep-seated desire to beat on certain individuals: the semi-literate school board president; the principal, recently promoted to superintendent, who thought that God was created in his very own image (how quickly administrators forget that they were once teachers) with all of his wheeling and dealing; the director who was into sibling rivalry and constantly attempting to outdo his politically successful brother. When God conceived of man and provided him with an anal orifice through which to pass waste, he must have used these guys as perfect working models; they all shared many negative qualities, but one thing stood out- they were people who loved most to criticize and condemn others while projecting themselves as the watchdogs/pillars of the community's better interest. No doubt, they did this to increase their own self-importance which amounted to nothingness anyway. I longed for retribution and revenge...

The saga continues with yours truly in an extremely volatile and dangerous state; following a very embarrassing situation which involved considerable damage to a new 280Z automobile that was inflicted by my forearm as well as my stupidity, I reasoned that I'd better shape up before I did something really off-the-wall! I was really out of control and in jeopardy of being thrown in the slammer if my behavior continued on its downward spiral; therefore, after having a very serious discussion with the looking-glass, I made the committment or resolution to redirect my negative energies that were being wasted on foolish emotionalism; I was determined from that point forward to not give into those low-lives with the self-pity garbage because this was precisely what they wanted!

This is what occurred that Friday night; I went out in an attempt to escape my sorry fate and my negative state of mind. Together with some friends, we sallied forth to a local watering hole known as Barney's where the clientele was fun, the drinks good and potent, and the prices very reasonable. I'm afraid that I overindulged, not only in my own self-pity, but also with Southern Comfort Manhattans as well. We left Barney's about two hours later and God only knows how many Manhattans! Luckily, I wasn't driving and we decided to proceed to another local establishment known as the Pig Pen where we were hopeful that some lovelies may be awaiting our arrival with bated breath- well, hope can sometimes prove consolable. In any event, I met and ended up with a girl by the name of Joycelyn who possessed a very hard, fine body. I recall that the following approach worked out quite well. You should ask the person to slow dance and while you're moving suggestively "dirty", you whisper the following:

"I would very much like to be alone with you right now- in a dark room somewhere so that we could get into comparative anatomy by braille." You either got hit or they'd laugh and you'd score because they'd appreciate your sense of humor. If you were lucky, you could possibly end up in that dark room; I ended up in her dark car, out in the equally dark parking lot. We were all over each other and approaching the meltdown stage when Joycelyn asked me if I had any cocaine on me because she wanted to "heighten the experience."

"I know that you have 'coke' because somebody in the bar told me that she heard you $old the stuff."

ALmost instantly, I went limp; she was nothing but a coke slut and I got really pissed off; where were people getting this shit; I detested everything and anything that had to do with drugs; they represented the antithesis of all that I stood for. I also became painfully aware of the fact that I had consumed too much alcohol (a dangerous drug) that night. The timing was all wrong and I completely lost it. I simply wanted out, so I opened the door, got out and foolishly forearmed her new front door all of the way to the front wheelwell. The window shattered into 1,000 pieces and I bent the door frame, also. This little fiasco cost me muchos dolares on that fateful night, I was never so disappointed in myself!

In order to maintain my cool, I once again turned to long distance running and sketching; I proved to be far better than I had thought possible.

Chapter 16:

"Deciding on Priorities"

I had become almost immune to physical pain of any kind; I was logging between 65-70 miles a week in preparation for my second Boston Marathon. Theoretically speaking, one was supposed to steadily increase one's mileage over a 12 week span; however, I had only 6 weeks in which to train since the weather and my schedule dictated otherwise. I became as flexible as possible under the adverse circumstances and continued training for what would prove to be another memorable experience in my life. Since the accomplishment of the latter, two other occurrences would have to outrank and outclass running the marathon-meeting my wife and sharing our love by having two beautiful sons for this was happiness in every sense of the word. Well, let me regress again to the training and eventual running of the race before I digress any further.

My primary motivation in wanting to run the race a second time was quite simple; I wondered if it were physically possible for me to run such a great distance in a fixed period of time. I knew from the previous year that I could finish. I had always been a chronic asthmatic; throughout my life I understood, but resented, my limitations as well as my parents overly protective attitude involving my participation in strenuous, demanding sports; therefore, I suppose that's why I elected to participate in football, wrestling, and marathons. Besides the obvious disadvantage of having asthma, I was also quite large for a marathoner since I weighed 185 pounds and was 5 ft. 11 in. tall. In any event, at the conclusion of my fourth week of training, I had dropped weight to 167 pounds. I reasoned that no matter what evolved at Boston, I would finish the race in under 3 ½ hours and I certainly didn't want to wait until the twilight of my life to reflect on wishing that I had done something that I hadn't. At the very least when I'm ready for my rocking chair (I already possess the dog and the fireplace) I'll be able to reflect on realities, not on meaningless fantasies. I'm digressing again- toward the end of the fourth week, I put myself to a test, which normally should have come in the sixth week. I plotted out and ran a course that was about twenty miles in order to determine whether or not I could handle it; I made it! That was an unbelieveable, natural high, not obtainable chemically and I couldn't wait for April 26th. I was totally psyched and looking forward to the race with great anticipation. Ten of us were supposed to travel to Boston together, but as it turned out, I had to talk someone into running the race with me; the other nine guys proved to be all talk, all barroom philosophers because they never made the trip.

Arriving to the starting line at about 11:50, I buried myself in the rear of the pack; my philosophy was three-fold: finish the race, do it nonstop and under three and a half hours, and finally try to pass as many runners as possible who had been given official numbers because they had previously qualified in under three hours.

To reiterate, I had run the race the previous year, but my

time was in the four hour range and I had stopped to walk on six different occasions during the race. What a beautiful experience it turned out to be; wall-to-wall spectators, all of whom seemed to really care, and all of whom proved to be a constant source of encouragement and motivation by offering drinks, oranges, and all kinds of support.

The runners began to separate at about the five mile mark, and I was beginning to run very comfortably; at the fourteen mile point I felt very strong and was averaging about 7:04 minutes per mile; suddenly, I made an abrupt right hand turn and found myself scaling the fabled Heartbreak Hill. I was approaching the halfway point on the hill when something happened to me which I shall never forget. One of the wheelchair competitors- they are normally finished before the top runners because their competition is completed first- had evidently entered his first race and was in the process of "hitting the wall." He seemed to be experiencing a great deal of pain, but he refused to give in and quit. Tears were streaming down his face which appeared to be distorted by the strain. Not realizing that I had been running alongside of him for about ten minutes in sheer admiration and respect, my body and mind began to play games with one another; I started hurting myself because placing one foot in front of the other became an effort and I wanted to walk for a while. It would have been so easy to stop and do just that; I looked at the guy beside me and was immediately disgusted with my negative attitude. We began to talk. Following introductions, Scott confirmed what I had suspected, in that, he had injured his left wrist and was experiencing some pain; he told me that he didn't think that he would be able to hold on to finish but I tried to convince him that he could and that I was going to make certain that we both finished! Scott's guts and spirit really got my adrenaline pumping; it was as though our encounter had been predetermined because without each other's verbal abuses and encouragement, neither one would have made it to the top and completed the race.

Politics, nepotism, hypocrisy, and school boards with all of their negative bullshit didn't matter worth a damn because at that moment in time, they ceased to exist. I wondered to myself and to Scott aloud how many other people may have been fortunate enough at some point in their lives to truly appreciate and to understand what life really had to offer-the true meaning that can only be grasped through a similar experience. We two friends, in this time and place, finished the race and celebrated our mutual achievement; words once more fall short in conveying the inner-peace and spirituality of the moment. The faith in my fellow man so long absent as well as the idealism that I once possessed, we rekindled; all of the sacrifice, all of the sweat and toil must have been necessary in order to attain this knowledge, and the wisdom that went with it.

My bitterness toward the conspirators had pretty much left me, and I could only feel sorry for them because they had obviously wasted their lives on the small town mentality of political intrigue which was so lacking in both merit and morality. I'm convinced that when they "kick off", they're in big trouble with the Man.

Following the marathon, I decided to do some independent research regarding faculty seniority and discovered that there would be an opening in the English department due to a pending retirement. Being somewhat hopeful, but skeptical as well, I registered for graduate classes at my alma mater; I was informed that I had missed the first two weeks of classes and that I would undoubtedly have a great deal of work to make up- what else is new? To become certified I would have to take three courses (9 credits) and it would be necessary to be inserted into classes which had small enrollments; it didn't take long to figure out why there were so few people in these classes- they were very demanding professors and the courses that they were teaching seemed extremely challenging, and Art Whiteknight happened to be two weeks later to register for said classes, but that was because I hadn't discovered about the retirement soon enough.

I won't bore you with all of the gorey details of that memorable summer, and of the academic pressures involved in attempting to make up two weeks of missed classes; needless to say, my social life ceased to exist and based upon the aforementioned encounter with the 280Z, perhaps it was just as well! Thank God for the advent and popularity of distance running because if I didn't have that as a therapy, I know for a fact that survival would have been next to impossible under those circumstances.

There were some very positive things which occurred that summer as well; I was afforded the opportunity of meeting some very interesting, wonderful people, one of whom was probably the most intelligent human being I've ever known. We got to be close friends and I shared my dilemma; she cared and offered some sound, objective advice regarding my possible options- she helped me tremendously in so many different ways...

Fortunately, I earned an A, a B+, and a B; the sense of relief was awesome; I had achieved what at first seemed another impossible task, but, to reiterate, I've always been of the opinion that some of the greatest "highs" in life involved realizing something that most people deem to be beyond your capabilities or potential. Meanwhile, people were asking questions like: "Why the hell even bother; are you a masochist or what; isn't it aggravating enough that these clowns, who think that they rule you, have spit in your face and now you want to go back for more? What's wrong with you? Man, you'd be better off somewhere else!"

You see, what they failed to realize was that they (the power brokers) had to be dealt with seriously and a precedent had to be established so that this particular scenario wouldn't be repeated; after all, what other options did I have at this point? I could allow myself to be ridiculed privately as well as publically which would lead people to the erroneous conclusion that I was incompetent, negligent, and morally suspect; or, I could fight them "tooth and nail" to reestablish, once and for all, my character and the dignity that stands behind character; I also had the golden opportunity to expose those misguided individuals for the lowly phonies that they were, yet again- a final assault. Thank the Man upstairs with the big 'G' on his sweatshirt, I had them in an embarrassing, uncompromising position. It was definitely at the "check mate" stage in the chess game which they were responsible for initiating.

Believe it or not, the fearless leaders had done many foolish things, but one stands out uppermost in mind; they had hired someone for the vacated English position without adhering to the union's contractual provisions which stated that: "All vacancies must be posted for a period of 30 days prior to said vacancy being filled; further, that preference for the opening be given to anyone within the bargaining unit who happened to be qualified." Ah, there was the rub!

Once again, they had hired "one of their own" to fill the vacancy; this oversight would prove to be their downfall, or at least I had hoped that it would. There was almost a comedic element involved this time; it's difficult to believe but the individual that they hired (John Pawn) had not yet been certified in education. He would have to be granted an emergency certificate and would have a time limitation in order to earn his accreditation. It didn't take a great deal of intelligence to put 2+2 together and to figure out that I was presently far more qualified than he could ever hope to be. He may have been qualified and the Board contrived this excuse in order to attempt saving face once again; after all, they now had egg drop soup smeared all over their collective countenances. In any event, I grieved the appointment and with all of the humility I could possibly muster (while grinning from ear to ear) I made my grandiose entrance into the superintendent's inner-sanctum. You can't possibly imagine the sense of deep-felt satisfaction that I was experiencing, nor could you fathom Sir Marionette's facial expressions and accompanying body language which reflected an intense animation! He was not a happy camper; his chin fell to his knees when he saw my state certification in English which had been added to my teaching certificate. Every blessed second of trial and tribulation that I had suffered through had been more than worth it! The picture had been worth 1,000,000 words!! My character and integrity had been restored while theirs was brought into question; how could anyone doubt or even debate that fact?! THEY HAD GIVEN IT THEIR BEST SHOT, and I HAD GIVEN IT MINE; I, HOWEVER, WAS ALRUISTIC AND MORAL AND THEY OBVIOUSLY WEREN'T.

Not only had I regained my coaching positions, but the threatened loss of employment, had also been totally negated; everyone knows that you just can't beat city hall... remember? I kept thinking of Jackie Gleason's favorite line- how truly sweet it was... Marionette offered his hand replete with a profound and sensitive comment: "Let's let bygones be bygones"; we were burying the proverbial hatchet, although, I can't quite recall ever having done anything malicious or underhanded to him. A consumation devoutly to be wished for, finally realized; it was absolutely great as well as fulfilling!

The only flaw that surfaced involved the vote on re-hiring me as the wrestling coach; the intellectual Board president had played the stereotypical fool once more by casting the only dissenting ballot; his rationale was based upon some of that solicited evidence which had been dismissed during the arbitration as being inadmissable... the vote stood, however, at eight in favor and one opposed.

Chapter 17:

"Mixed Reactions"

Once September rolled around, the varying reactions of my fellow teachers proved to be rather interesting, sometimes even amusing; they ranged from, "Gee, you're like a bad penny, they can't seem to get rid of you, no matter how hard they try." to "I'm really happy for you and for everyone you may have indirectly helped; they'll think twice before they consider trying to ruin or defame someone else's character- you really showed them, you definitely outsmarted them!"

The exploited individuals who didn't help my cause at all by submitting drivel and by allowing themselves to be browbeaten tried to make amends; I suppose that whatever consciences or scruples they had remaining were stinging a bit. Although the overall reaction was by far a positive one, I did sense feelings of envy and jealousy in some of them. I imagine that in my situation, most of them would have lain down and played dead; these individuals were the people who were busy jumping on the bandwagon and claiming that my career in coaching and education had been terminated before it actually had a chance to begin. May I say again that I enjoyed "sticking it" in their collective ears!

There weren't any immediate or direct reprisals,

however, there were ever-present undertones; the new principal (Samuel Silverspoon) proved to be anything but an enigma. He became infamous for his documentation as well as his "see me's" regarding whatever triviality; in any event, he rubbed me the wrong way from day one. What disturbed me most about him was that he was constantly trying to project himself as being something/someone that he most certainly wasn't- fair! During the proceedings of our first encounter, he contradicted himself by saying in one breath that he had heard conflicting stories about me, some very good and others equally bad. He, however, in his magnanimous way, would attempt to judge me fairly.

"Nevertheless, Mr. Whiteknight, you had better watch yourself carefully and closely because you'll be scrutinized and put under the microscope, so be prepared; it's nothing personal, I assure you. I'm simply following instructions from above."

Gee, what a fair man, I thought, on exiting his office. I had become somewhat curious when I discovered that this wonderfully just human being had come to us by way of the N.E. Connection, Vito Correlieon, the resident mayor in one of the communities which comprised the district; this buck also happened to be Silverspoon's brother-in-law. How coincidental and convenient, right?! The selection was quite odd, in that, there were more qualified people within the school district. The Board, however, in their ultimate wisdom passed them over in favor of the import, one Samuel Silverspoon- it was so blatantly obvious that it actually reeked! As my little investigation continued, it became clear that the new principal had secured the inside track because his wife shared the very same bloodline as our good friend Vito who had also been recently appointed president of the school board. Dastardly nepotism had scored once more!

Qualifications, recommendations, grade transcripts, and merit had absolutely little, if anything, to do with important decision-making situations; what mattered most around this area was who you knew politically, whose family you married into, or whose ass you might be willing to kiss to get "ahead". If your qualifications were outrageously superior, they would manage to rationalize their choice or perhaps even "lose" your application.

Well, Mr. Silverspoon showed himself for the chump that he would prove to be early on, for there developed the chosen ones, a clique which he championed and favored; they eventually became known among us peons as the Golden Boys. It's sad, sorry, but also a reality. It had everything to do with the concept of favoritism as the terms applies to the human condition; preferential treatment of every conceivable kind was afforded to a handful of people who found themselves in the good graces of the Board for whatever reason; again, the reason usually involved family or political connections. I don't mean to "beat a dead horse", but it was another classic example of the hackneyed observation "history usually repeats itself in a negative sense".

Chapter 18:
"Mellowing Out- in Retrospection"

Quite a few years have transpired since these events unfolded in my life, and I would like to think that I've become less bitter, less cynical- at least to some extent. Unfortunately, however, politics (as usual) continues to rear it's ugly head in all matters with all too great a frequency. The catharsis experienced while participating in the Boston Marathon has transformed itself into a cynical realism; in other words, I still haven't learned to "play the game" but I have learned how to cope in order to maintain some degree of sanity; that may not be an acceptable or commendable approach, however, it has made survival somewhat more tolerable. I still maintain that the education of children represents a sacred pilgrimage and should definitely be off limits to small-time politicians and their inane games and mentalities. The insensitive and often inhumane arena of politics should be forever severed from the hallowed halls of education. Human lives and reputations should never be considered expendable or exploitive commodities.

Machiavellianism, which denies the relevance of morality while valuing cunning and deceit, can not be condoned or justified on any grounds because it's inherently unethical and decadent in every respect... of course, anyone who's naive enough to think that the situation may change for the better might as well have Scotty beam them up or back in time to 16th century England to hold meaningful discourse with Sir Thomas More regarding his Utopian fantasies. Hey! Sometimes you do have to wonder if there are any truly intelligent life forms on this earth...What the hell- I'm only asking for a minor miracle or something along those lines!! I must be upfront and admit to the fact that the bitterness has resurfaced, although not with the same intensity; once again history has repeated itself, etc...

Some theoretical bureaucrats (in their ultimate wisdom) devised and labeled an interesting catch-all phrase commonly referred to as "teacher burnout". Well, my interpretation goes something like this- in a very personal sense, I submit that the students may not always be the primary cause of this syndrome. Consider, for instance, the example of a previously narrated scenario: the new principal assures you that he intends to be more than fair and equitable regarding all interpersonal dealings; then, as the days, weeks and months unfold, he transforms himself into a one man jury focused on a guilty verdict... guilty with not even a remote chance of innocence. This character (Silverspoon) proceeded to observe my classroom no less than ten times within a three month span. Most assuredly, he was being more than fair by monitoring my classes with such uncharacteristic zeal. I informed the twit that I intended to file harassment charges through the union president if he continued with the nonsense. I could only surmise that one of his "masters" must have told him to continue the harassment because I had beaten them on three separate occasions. Talk about poor sportsmanship! Principal Silverspoon attempted to justify his frequent observations through rationalization; since I would now be teaching English and not French, he deemed it purely logical that he took it upon himself to "facilitate" my transition into the new subject area so that any unforeseen problems might be quickly and easily resolved.

God, he was so ingenuine and unprofessional that I almost gagged; this pompous, little pawn's vision didn't extend beyond the tip of his nose. Therefore, I decided to be as blunt and tactless with him by reading him the riot act and reminding Mr. "Fair" that so long as he was dealing with all members of the faculty in the same fashion, he could continue with his good intentioned observations; otherwise, Sir Fairman would have to cease and desist unless he chose to live-on-the-edge and to risk failure in yet a fourth grievance submitted on the grounds of harassment.

The pompous ass must have thought that he could intimidate me because he possessed political as well as nepotistic connections on the infamous Board- what a small, shallow man he proved to be. What a grave disappointment he eventually became to the entire faculty, some of whom thought him to be a wonderful person upon first arrival.

"Mr. Whiteknight, based upon my classroom observations, I would have to say that you're doing a fine job, however, I must inject a word of caution and advice because of my concern."

"Well, Mr. Silverspoon, what might that be?"

"Please understand that you have caused a good amount of embarrassment to certain influential people on the Board and within the school itself."

"I beg to differ with you, Mr. Silverspoon, but, on the contrary, they're the ones who are directly responsible for any 'black eyes' that they may have suffered. Just to get to the point; don't attempt being subtle now because it's much too late for that."

"Yes, well, they, or rather we, would prefer that you continue doing a commendable job in the classroom, and it may be more prudent on your part if you wouldn't choose to re-apply for either of the coaching positions, despite the fact that we are supposed to reinstate you."

"Surely, you jest; Mr. S., I've gone to hell and back in order to regain those coaching positions and if you people think that you're going to intimidate or dump on me again, you're sorely mistaken. Do what you have to do, but as far as I'm concerned this conversation is terminated. Talk about Mickey Mouse meadow muffins! Whenever you want to pursue this subject any further, the union president will definitely be present. I've had more than my fill... Who in the hell do you think you are anyway?! I'm out of here, Mr.' Fair' ."

The preceding experience provides great insight and meaning to my previous observation regarding the interpretation of that universal "teacher burnout" thing. How can people be so void or vacant of sensitivity, compassion, ethics, morality and all of the other wonderful Godly attributes we humans are supposed to reflect and practice? Why is there such a concerted focus on theory, idealism and morality in college because these inspiring concepts are usually cast aside in the real world. What matters most in terms of priorities is that which is politically expedient or acceptable... and that's a very sad commentary; as a matter of fact, it can actually become quite depressing and shameful, but, then, I happen to possess one of those awful things known as a conscience. What should be and what actually exists- why does one seem to be the antithesis of the other? Sometimes I become so damn frustrated! Bookwork and theory are often seriously lacking in practical application... What the hell- like the commercial states, "why ask why?" Can ignorance actually be blissful? Stew Stabeck used to think so...

Risking eternal optimism again, why shouldn't people in education be promoted on their merit and qualifications; why aren't teachers treated like professionals and appreciated; why aren't all sports and athletes/scholars treated equally because they all deserve our support and encouragement; and why is it usually the case that the people who would make the best administrators remain in the classroom in an attempt to make a real difference?

I have been giving a great deal of thought to the vertical mobility thing because of my wife's financial woes; I'm very much preoccupied by the reality that I won't be able to finance my sons' college education unless I move on to "bigger and better" salaried positions available in administration. I, undoubtedly, should have made the move about ten years ago- perhaps thirteen, before the birth of my oldest son!

What can I say, only that I consumately detest Cromwellian political cronies like Silverspoon, Marionette and people like them; perhaps I fear becoming "tainted" myself...

Speaking of politics, whoever devised the idea for the modern-day Board of Education anyway? Many of these people have no clue about what's significant regarding education's trials and tribulations; and, yet, they're entrusted with the monumental task of setting things right! Many of these individuals possess honorable intentions but there are many who don't. Sometimes they may spend as much as $5,000 or more to be elected into a non-salaried position; they sacrifice many hours and a considerable amount of stress and aggravation, but to what end? Are there sometimes ulterior motives and hidden agendas beneath the surface?

The unfortunate but honest response to the latter is a resounding "yes". The school board has evolved into nothing more than the reflection of the larger macrocosm of politics, replete with all of its flaws and its Machiavellian philosophies which transform principles into compromise, untruths into diplomacy, and merit or qualifications into empty, meaningless words...

Is this all our country and our so-called democracy has become? Why should a man who's already quite wealthy seek to increment that wealth illegally and at the expense of our children's education by unfairly securing roofing contracts for his own bogus company? Why must people be so greedy and decadent, especially when innocent kids and their futures are involved? It makes me want to chuck my cookies!

I have grown rather cynical and somewhat disillusioned about many aspects of life: petty, political school boards, administrators who forget their classroom experiences and roots all too quickly and metamorphosize into empty and spiritless "yes men"; disloyal people; parents who don't and never will give a damn about anything meaningful, namely their children; arrogant, snotty students who fancy they know it all but, realistically speaking, are aware of very little at best; holier than thou peers who $ell their souls for all of the wrong reasons in an attempt to score "brownie points" in the hope of personal advancement; most pathetic and depressing, however, are those kids who are completely negative toward everyone and everything, kids who don't learn and can't comprehend what's real because they've never acquired the necessary reading levels or skills. They've been simply passed on and forgotten. They possess serious reading deficiencies and become intensely alienated and/or hostile because the core material is no longer exciting or challenging; rather, it's a source of embarrassment and anxiety. They continue to be awarded by promotion; however, they should be provided an environment free from stigma and ridicule to overcome their deficiencies so that the educational process can once again become enjoyable and rewarding, as well as meaningful. Guidance departments had better start listening more closely through dialogs with the classroom teachers who are desperate for help and assistance with these educational "misfits"; we can't continue sweeping them under the carpet and the situation must be resolved at the earliest age possible!

I don't mean to sound Arian, but parents who aren't willing and able to accept the weighty responsibility of bringing children into the world and providing them with the necessary love and sensitivity, shouldn't really be blessed with children. Lately, it seems that most of our transfers come to us physically and/or mentally scarred due to their unstable, dysfunctional family environments. It's tragically sad and so unnecessary. Sterility might sound too calloused but sometimes it would be a justifiable alternative to bringing children who will be severely abused and psychologically destroyed (in one way or another) into this world...

Nevertheless, there's a flicker of hope and idealism somewhere because many of us persevere through teaching or coaching in the hope that we can, no, we do make a difference! We may be motivated by a single essay which reflects and affirms the fact that somewhere, somehow, this student was inspired and, therefore, cared enough to give something back in respect or appreciation; the letters which will follow are a living testament to the latter insight.

In my particular case, I suppose that the glass will always be half full as opposed to half empty... this book serves as an affirmation of that hope and love which tend to keep yours truly coming back for more. People have often questioned me regarding my reasons/rational with respect to remaining in teaching in consideration of all of the negatives that I've confronted over the span of some 25 years in the profession. The following anecdote and letters will answer that question far more definitively and eloquently than I ever could. Also, included is a final dedication and thank you to one of the most influential people that I've ever had the great fortune to have known.

Chapter 19:
"Thankful and Blessed-Why Teach?"

The year was 1990 and the place was Williamsport, Pennsylvania. One of my wrestlers had realized a first, and one of those seemingly unattainable goals; he became our first Regional Champion. What made the achievement amazingly significant was the fact that he had participated in the sport for only three years. We had taken showers and were preparing to go to a restaurant in order to "pig out".

At this point, I must make you aware of some pertinent facts regarding Richard's home life which was pretty much nonexistent except for a hard-working mother, and a good-hearted uncle who attempted to be there as much as possible for Richard. Unfortunately, Sal couldn't make it to Regionals because he was experiencing some serious problems in his own life (a painful divorce). The greatest quality about Richard had nothing to do with his athletic prowess (He was 6'2, 260 pounds and a three sport all-star); rather, it had everything to do with his sensitivity and the fact that he was such an outstanding human being in, oh, so many ways!

I sensed that Richard seemed very nervous and

uncomfortable; I asked him why?

"Richard, why are you so damned 'uptight' and standing there staring at me? Do I have a booger hanging down or what? Is there something bothering you?"

"Well, yeah, Coach there is something, but I don't want you to take this the wrong way! I don't know if I can bring myself to do this, and, if I can, I know that I won't be able to express it properly."

"What is it, please don't be so self-conscious about it and talk to me. When did we ever have any trouble talking to each other?"

"Well, here goes then, Coach, I don't want you to get the wrong impression of me or anything. You know that I really care about and like Teresa, but I don't really feel love for her, yet."

"For God's sake, will you please look at me and tell me what's on your mind!"

"OK, OK just remember that I'm not gay or anything but…"

He proceeded to hug me and I reciprocated; he told me that I meant a great deal to him, and that I was always there for him when others weren't; that he had not only learned a great deal about discipline and sacrifice but, more importantly, a great deal more about life and his own potentials. Finally, in tears he observed that he never had a "real" father but that I was like one to him and that he grew to love me for that reason; he thanked me for everything; he said that he would never forget me.

What the hell, how do you respond to something like that? The tears welled up and I melted. There we were, two big brutes reduced to tears, hugging each other. I responded that I loved him as well and that I would always continue to be there for him whenever he needed me. Andy, my assistant, happened to walk into the room at that moment and in his typical smart ass style asked us if we wanted him to leave so that we could be alone? Richard grabbed him and hugged him as well!

We sallied forth into the night, found a great restaurant and proceeded to stuff our faces. Vic, one of my former wrestlers who I could have claimed as a dependent at one point and time, offered to foot the bill and, of course, Richard and I unwillingly condescended.

In 25 years of teaching and coaching, this night had to be the most touching and memorable of so many positive experiences... This constitutes the very reason why teaching/coaching are such honorable and worthy professions. Experiences like the latter have kept me not only motivated, but also fulfilled, and all of the politics in the world could never take away the accomplishments or the cherished experiences which will sustain me for the remainder of my life... thank you, God, for all of the tremendous kids that I've taught and coached!

(Following are Richard's parting words scribed into the year book, 1990 edition):

"Thanks to a fantastic coach, Mr. Whiteknight, for being an inspiration and for teaching me everything worthwhile in life. If it weren't for you, my achievements wouldn't be possible. Always in memory, Richard..."

(Insert the two letters)

Chapter 20:

"In Passing"

Over the passage of some seventeen years, despite the lack of encouragement and only token support, the wrestling program has accrued 96 tournament champions, 13 Outstanding Wrestler Awards at these tournaments, 12 District champs, Regional champs and place winners, as well as 8 State qualifiers/place winners.

My assistant and I have also been honored by the press and, more significantly, by our peers- the true measure of achievement. Additionally, during the decade of the 80s, our teams had, without the benefit of a feeder program (elementary or junior high) or facility (wrestling room), managed to win over 78% of their dual meets, finished in the black financially thanks to decent crowds, and succeeded in bringing nothing but honor and prestige to reflect our school district in a very positive light.

Sadly, however, the future bodes anything but brightly; the last four years have proven disappointing and frustrating since we're presently in a downward slide in terms of student involvement and winning tradition; our teams are now winning barely 25% of their duals. It's a bloody shame but no one seems to give a damn except for the kids who participate, their coaches, and a handful of former wrestlers who are attempting to organize a supportive "political" entity- yes, that dirty word rears its ugly head- and, lastly, a small number of concerned parents.

When I coached golf during the 70s, the kids managed some rather remarkable achievements and I was fortunate to garner several coaching honors, also. We earned five consecutive League Championships, were undefeated and untied during the last two years, succeeded in winning in excess of 91% of our matches (82-8-1) secured 21 League All-Stars, 6 District champions, and had one young man finish 17th in the State competition.

The real tragedy and travesty is that majority members of the power structure within the school system have chosen to continue their petty revenge obsession against me at the expense of the kids that I coach. They're presently contemplating dropping the wrestling program if numbers don't return to what they used to be. It's partly the resultant frustration which ultimately helped to motivate me to write this book and to share this story. God willing, something positive and hopeful may eventuate in order to eliminate the present abuses. There must always be hope!!

The book represents a testament to the fact that when you set goals and dream dreams, you must let your reach always exceed your grasp and whatever it may be you strive to attain, reach for the stars and persevere. When you begin realizing your potentials, you become aware that the so-called unattainable can be realized but only by maintaining a bulldog-like tenacity to hang in there and overcome whatever the obstacles may be... perseverance can change attitudes, and when you attain the unattainable, your life will become rich and full; the resulting confidence and self-esteem will inspire you toward greater and more noble endeavors. The word "can't" should be removed from the English language; don't allow yourself to be manipulated by self-imposed limitations- carpe diem, my friend... cease the day, capture the moment...

Chapter 21:

"Suggestions and Perceptions"

Reflecting on my experiences in the teaching and coaching professions, I would like to offer my observations and suggestions which hopefully might catalyze a significant/constructive change for the better if instituted in place of the present quandary. The status quo is a system which seems to be deteriorating with each passing year. What follows, then, is a sharing of concerns, observations and possible solutions to the problems presently confronting public education, an eight-step plan, if you will:

1. First and foremost would involved changing the composition of the school board. As alluded to previously in the book, many directors who are elected have no knowledge about the truly significant issues facing education; many happen to be local politicians who become directors simply because of their familiarity or popularity in the community. Some of them may even have hidden agendas.

    Since there's probably no escaping the present democratic process of election, the candidates should be carefully evaluated and their qualifications stipulated. They should meet the following criteria and be screened by a selection committee composed of school administrators, teachers, professionals and clergy from the community before they're even allowed to be candidates.

A. They shouldn't hold any other political office or harbor any political ambitions; allowing some local politicians to run might prove to be as foolish as letting a diabetic kid loose in a candy store. They should, therefore, be purist and altruistic since this individual will be directly responsible for our children's educational opportunities and futures.

B. A candidate should possess some degree of working knowledge regarding significant educational issues, other than teacher's salaries. It seems that directors are constantly ready to blame teacher salaries on millage increases. They invariably never have enough money for the people in "the trenches" whose efforts produce high quality education; but they have plenty for administrators. I've grown weary of the teacher-bashings; good teachers/coaches should once again be respected as well as appreciated. They should learn this respect at home, so parents should dispense with the scorn and sarcasm.

C. A candidate should possess management skills, business acumen of some sort, a working familiarity of the school code and laws (a lawyer perhaps), a minimum of five years teaching experience, or should be a representative from the clergy. The number combinations could be discussed and resolved.

This eclectic approach would prove to be far superior to the present political, popularity contests that are presently perpetuating mediocrity or failure at best!

2. The educational "misfits" must be identified at an early age and these low-level readers must be encouraged and taught to acquire the skills necessary to promote a positive attitude toward learning and academics. Let's be realistic, how can someone enjoy or appreciate what he/she can't understand nor comprehend? The majority of academically successful students usually happen to be better than average writers; additionally, gifted writers are normally avid readers. Education has to be a fun, learning experience.

3. Teachers are "accountable" and rightfully so; parents have to become more accountable also in supporting and encouraging their kids, whether it's in academics or in athletic competition. When your kids need you, you should be there for them by helping them with homework (especially in the formative years), attending games/matches, or simply by listening and offering options when situations become too stressful... You should also teach your children that with increased responsibility, they will earn more freedom and trust. Lastly, teach them that respect isn't simply a song sung by soul sister, Aretha Franklin-this is extremely important.

One more thought, kids have only one childhood and one adolescence; earning extra money for car insurance, spending money or whatever are fine, worthy undertakings, but when parents pressure their kids to work at regular jobs and at the expense of denying them social involvement or athletic competition, then the employment idea is inherently wrong. Kids are afforded the opportunity to be kids only once in a lifetime...

4. Administrators should remain "in touch" with their faculties and students; they shouldn't shut themselves in their offices to become glorified paper-shufflers. They must remain people-oriented, be supportive toward teachers and attempt to commend as much as they criticize; they should also recall their roots and should earn their positions of responsibility based solely on qualifications and merit.

5. Teachers and coaches must strive to be more creative/ imaginative in their respective venues so that students may become more involved because they are more challenged; therefore, there should be less of a bookish, theoretical approach and more hands-on application: i.e. software in a consumer math class dealing with purchasing a house or balancing a budget; writing and art portfolios etc. Teachers must try to incorporate quality and relevance into the lesson plan.

6. The board of education and administration must institute parity among all sports; if it costs over $100,000 per year to simply maintain one facility while another sport has no facility whatsoever, something is very wrong somewhere!

7. The great American dream should be rekindled and guidance should have the responsibility of enlightening students regarding the projections of educational and career opportunities relative to the job market. There are too many people graduating from college after busting their humps for 4 to 6 years who can't find employment.

8. Last but not least, the Pennsylvania Interscholastic Athletic Association must intervene and do something similar to what the NCAA does during championship competitions regarding steroid detection and monitoring; steroid abuse is definitely on the rise and the PIAA must arrive to the realization that this serious problem is initiated in high school and intensifies in college!

Potential behavioral problems and life-threatening psychological addictions might be alleviated through a two-pronged attack by combining detection with education. Kids are being altered; kids are dying!!!

Chapter 22:
"A Final Dedication (Father Gannon)"

When I first met Father Gannon, I was somewhat intimidated by his obvious intellectual prowess, but also more impressed by his teaching skills in motivating his students to think and to express their thoughts and emotions into words through the creative medium of the essay.

He also made all of us aware of how truly transitory and precious life can be, and that we are but brief moments in the sun. Therefore, we should strive toward quality as well as meaning in our lives; and that we should make an attempt at leaving something of ourselves behind to benefit our fellow man when we are no longer a part of this world. To suggest Father Gannon was supremely interesting would be grossly understating his spell-binding, God-given ability to excite and inspire his students toward realizing potentials of which they weren't even aware!

I suppose that you could say we hit-it-off and took an immediate liking to one another; he would share insights by scribing comments on my papers; he would converse with me at lunch; and he would often call me at home in an effort to convert me to Catholicism because he felt (based upon the reading of my essays and my philosophy) that I was put here on this earth to help those less fortunate, and what better way, than through the priesthood? I kept insisting that he was mistaken in that respect because I wasn't Catholic, I eventually wanted a family at some point in my life, and, most importantly, I loved women. I would meet somebody with whom to share my love (Patricia), witness the miracle of life in the birth of two beautiful sons; I'm probably closer to the priesthood now than ever before because my eight-year-old sleeps between us quite often; Mason tends to foster unwanted celibacy and priestly thoughts!

Father Gannon certainly left a wonderful legacy, for he was, and always will remain, the greatest and most inspirational teacher I've ever had the good fortune of knowing. He was also a friend and is sorely missed. Father G., I hope that I've made you proud…

"Father Edward Gannon was a most unique individual. Here was a man and we may not see his like again. He had beautiful ambitions and fulfilled them. His time went to anyone who asked and though he possessed many friends, everyone of them became special and he gave himself to each as if that one alone mattered… the only thing that truly mattered to Father Gannon was to touch lives, for to touch lives was to touch hearts…"

*Delivered by Rev. William B. Hill, S.J. at Saint Peters Cathedral, Scranton, PA: Monday, April 28, 1986…

(Father Gannon): "Young people have to see their value reflected in our eyes. Only then can they begin to believe in themselves…"

Born: November 12, 1914
Ordained: June 18, 1944
Called Home: April 24, 1986

Dear Mr. Whiteknight:

You probably don't remember me. My married name is Kim Scitchfeld, but when you taught my ninth grade 5th period English class, I was Kim White. That was over ten years ago, making this long overdue.

I was very quiet, hardly ever speaking up in class. It was easier to communicate through my writing, which I loved. Not having much support from my family (at the time) made me insecure about most of what I did. You, though, saw something in me. I remember you once reading aloud something that I had written. As is normal for kids of that age, mostly everyone in the class was laughing because you had singled that out. You told me they were making fun of me because what I had written was good. I still have some papers written for your class, including my first term paper. These things mean nothing to anyone but me, but to me they are very special.

You were always so encouraging to me. You had a special way of caring for all your students that showed in just about everything you did. I felt a special kind of support with you such as I never felt with another teacher. You talked about the movie, "The Other Side of the Mountain", played "The Greatest Love of All" long before Whitney Houston recorded it and gave us a copy of "Your Children" from The Prophet. You may not remember any of this, but I'll never forget.

You were an inspiration to me; you made me want to be a writer. So I edited the school paper in my senior year, I constantly hoped that what I wrote would make you proud. I wanted to go on to college to study journalism, but my father didn't see the need to send me when in a few years I would be "married and having babies."

I spent six years doing secretarial work (hating it, of course), and now I am a full-time mother-by choice. I am very happy with my life now, and wouldn't trade my family for anything. I have not, however, given up the dream I have, and maybe someday I will be a writer.

I know that teaching must be a very frustrating profession; you have to deal with so many different types of kids, and an administrator that doesn't always seem to have their (or your) best interest at heart. I am hoping this note will somehow encourage you, that it will show you that you have made a difference in at least one life; my heart tells me there are many others, as well.

It may not seem like a "big deal" to hear from a full-time homemaker, and to tell the truth, I would much rather be enclosing my by-line from a newspaper or a copy of my book dedicated to you. However; that is not my position in life at the moment. My two boys are my top priority now, and I hope that I can instill in them the faith and confidence that you gave to me.

One thing that I remember clearly from your teaching is that you are an idealist. Even though you see the way things are, you also see the way that they should be. Never give this up, for this is the characteristic that helped you to see me not for the introverted girl I was, but for the person that I could be-the one I am still striving to become.

I have never written a note like this to a teacher, but you

have touched me. You have a God-given gift, you are a teacher who really cares and is not afraid to show it.

The word I keep seeing as I look this over is "special." You were very special to me. Thank you- everyone should have a teacher like you at least once in their life.

Sincerely,
Kim Scitchfeld

Dear Mr. Whiteknight

I want to thank you for your help and support this past semester. It helped to have someone who always believed in me on my side once again.

I recently heard that I received a scholarship from the Charlotte Newcome Foundation. I'm sure that your glowing letter of recommendation helped to sway the judges in my favor.

I hope that someday I will fulfill your vision of me as a teacher who makes a difference. And thanks for having such a selective memory. I remember being a much more annoying student than the Donna Maroni you wrote about.

Sincerely,
Donna

Chapter 23:
"A Decade of Regression"

Since I last scribed a word with respect to our less than exemplary school district, the political realm has strengthened its control further and any hope for a meaningful, healthy change has deteriorated greatly. Ten years have come and passed just as quickly; after thirty-three years of what most people would deem to be constructive as well as distinguished service as a teacher/coach, the quagmire got to be so stagnant and offensive that I was forced to reach a painful but necessary decision——retire, get the hell out in an attempt to maintain a semblance of personal dignity. Allow me to fill you in...

Our district proved to be unique in a myriad of ways; again, certain coaches and individuals belonged to the "Golden Boys" circle (the politically correct faction) and exhibited an open disdain and resentment toward any other coach who may have been successful in obtaining some positive press. You could actually sense their backstabbing in the hope that you would fail. They, the chosen few, craved so much for the local paper's ink that they reminded me of 'junkies' who were desperate to secure their next fix. It was totally shameless, immature and woefully unprofessional. So degrading and self-deprecating, even the student body perceived what was going on. The envy and jealousy fouled the air.

Two coaches, in particular, were notorious for verbally abusing other coaches and their programs. I can recall many incidents but there are two specific experiences, which provide glaring examples.

Nick Lossi was a wonderful teacher and a skilled coach/communicator; he also would have made a more profitable living as a standup comedian; for his storytelling, his special sense of humor and his timing in delivering a joke or a spontaneous rebuttal were priceless; Robin Williams, George Carlin, Chris Rock, Rodney Dangerfield——he would take a back seat to none of these pros. Over a thirty-year span, he attained a ton of honors and accolades by coaching three different sports; his teams garnered numerous district titles, regional championships, and state rankings. When coaching baseball and basketball, his teams were state runners-up. Whenever I would stop by his house in season, he would be in his basement (his dungeon) analyzing films in an attempt to focus on his opponent's weaknesses. The assistant principal, Mr. Perfecto, once coached the basketball team and fancied himself a Phil Jackson; he thrived on tooting his own horn and loved to dwell on his winning percentage; yet, he never came close to winning the big one, not even at the district level. At every opportunity he would degrade and badmouth the most successful basketball coach in the school's history.

"He has no clue what he is doing; I wish I had the opportunity to coach that team because we would have won states, not finished second. I, I, I, etc."

The 'part time' guidance counselor/football coach (Sam Stats) would not talk to the baseball coach, who preceded

Lossi because he gave the wrestling coach (yours turly) credit for helping to convert the smallest player on his team into a power hitter who lead the team in homeruns and RBI's. Nick approached Stats and confronted him by asking why he was receiving the cold shoulder?

"Bert, you mean to tell me that you really don't know why I am upset with you?"

"Sam I have no idea; what's the deal?"

"Well, why did you give that guy credit for anything, especially in the news paper? He's nothing but a pain in my ass; some of my best football players aren't lifting with the team because they would rather wrestle."

"Hey, Sam, maybe they are your best athletes because they wrestle."

"Besides, Justin (homerun & RBI leader on the baseball team) got tremendously strong since last year; pound for pound he's the strongest kid on my team. The only difference between last year and this season is the fact that he wrestled. The kid himself attributes this to Coach Whiteknight and wrestling."

"Bert, I have nothing more to say…"

Chapter 24:
"Educators or Demagogues?"

The school board through the democratic process had changed once again and the hope that existed regressed into hopelessness in the blinking of an eye; the guy they voted into the Presidency, Harry Giggalo, projected himself to be a pillar of the community and knowledgable about education——— Christ has risen! He turned out to be a chronic liar, hypocrite, adulterer; he lacked any and all saving human attributes.

Giggalo approached me in a local pub/eatery one night in order to share the following:

"You as a coach and wrestling in general have been screwed-over since day one in this district, and I want you to know that I will do anything I can to make things better, no matter what."

This was certainly surprising since Giggalo was one of Stat's (aforementioned football coach) cronies/disciples and constantly had his nose stuck up the latter's ass. Stats wanted his players in the weight room all year and he awarded the boys who gained the most weight and increased the poundage they lifted. This encouraged steroid abuse and it was common knowledge that six of the members of the '91 state championship team were 'users'. Stats would simply look the other way. This character thrived on control, intimidation, manipulation and exploiting the kids for all he could get out of them; he was a <u>hubris</u> freak who loved to hear himself referred to as the 'legend'.

I will return to Stats later…

Let's return to Harry Giggalo, our stellar board president. In his youth, he attended our school (Politico High) and was, at best, a mediocre athlete; however, he 'got off' in his role as volunteer-assistant coach by attempting to convince anyone who was naive enough to believe him that he was a great player. In reality, he was large, possessed very poor feet, and, even then, possessed a big mouth. The retrobate also fancied himself a Cassanova and repeatedly involved himself in extramarital affairs at the expense of his loving, overly forgiving wife who deserved so much better. The guy was essentially a sleeze-ball.

Some of my former wrestlers organized in a concerted effort to develop a political voice/edge and to initiate a movement in order to establish a viable junior high program which would insure the future of the sport at the school. We had always been a competitive program since day one, jumped head first into the league during the first year of the program's existence, and won over 75% of our dual meets following our second year in the league, despite not fielding a junior high team. Supposedly, the school lacked sufficient funds and couldn't justify the expense. The football program, however, received anything requested, no matter what the cost factor.

Nevertheless, the wrestling program produced 12 district champions, advanced 58 to regionals, and had multiple state place winners; more in fact, than any other team in the league. As far as I'm aware, this achievement was never matched in the state because all of the best programs throughout the state possessed, not only junior high teams that participated in competitive leagues, but also established leagues for elementary programs. We were at a blatant disadvantage from the program's inception.

Anyway, my former wrestlers exerted pressure by lobbying for a 'feeder', and a practice facility since we were forced to use the cafeteria for practice; talk about unsanitary! One of the wrestlers, who was a regional manager for a pharmaceutical company, assumed the leadership role. He phoned Giggalo in order to plead our case.

"Hello, Harry, this is Vic Tuffi. Do you have time to spare me a couple of minutes? Coach told me you may be interested in helping us in securing a practice area in the intermediate building."

"Hey, Vic, I was with your brother yesterday for a few brewskies at Friday's. I'd like to do whatever I can to help you guys out and to help build the program."

"How's your family?"

"Everyone's great, how about you?"

"Everything is fine. Listen, since you guys are in the process of drawing up plans for a new intermediate school, is there any chance that you could include an area to function as a multi-purpose room and possibly allocate some money for a junior high team?"

"Well, I'll do whatever I can to help out, Vic. I'll mention this in our next work session."

I personally attended the next public meeting to address the issue before the board members; I was loaded for bear, in that I presented actual floor plans and concrete solutions that would resolve any financial arguments vs. the proposals offered. Most of the expense for the practice facility would be covered and/ or reimbursed by state and federal aid since the room would be labeled as "multi-purposed" and students who were physically challenged would also be able to utilize the room. They (the Board) informed me that the proposal would receive serious consideration; the following week, however, I was summoned to the principal's office and was "summarily disciplined" for masterminding a plot to incite parents and students.

"Mr. Whiteknight, I received a disturbing phone call from a board member this morning and Mr. Giggalo claims that you personally pressured Mr. Tuffi into harassing him regarding the wrestling room issue. According to Harry, Vic's tone and attitude were ignorant as well as threatening; he also awakened his entire family."

"Mr. Sapp, I have no knowledge regarding content or tone, but I was aware of the fact that Vic might call Mr. Giggalo in order to gain some support; why don't you call Vic to get his side of the story? The man is a former student and regional manager for a large, well respected company; why would he risk or jeopardize his reputation by making such a call? I submit to you that someone isn't being upfront and honest here; please make the call to Vic."

"Oh, I didn't have the time in my busy schedule to do that."

"I can appreciate the fact that you may be in a bind time wise, but you allocated time for Giggalo; don't you think that Vic deserves the same courtesy? That's the only way you'll get to the bottom of this dilemma."

I walked out of Sapp's office and was given an apology six months later by Giggalo himself. There's an insight into Giggalo's lack of character and integrity.

Chapter 25:

"After Thoughts"

Harry Giggalo was caught quite literally with his "pants down" by his wife in his own driveway with his mistress. The latter was married with a family of her own, and she was appointed strength coach for the school district shortly thereafter; perhaps it had something more to do with her 'Clintonesque' oral techniques than with her qualifications or skills as a coach.

There wasn't any room in their relationship for discretion, for they met and displayed their carnal desires in very public environs; plumpish Liz was like Harry's trophy and a testament to his manliness. It's frightening to consider the repercussions that have transpired since the advent of Viagra. Giggalo (homo sapien erectus) was undoubtedly overdosing on "Pfizer's risers" on a daily basis. Hide the women and sheep, stud muffin is in the house. What a wonderful role model for everyone to emulate; what a low life loser...

"I'm President of the School Board at Politico High."

Prior to this incident, Harry carried on another affair with his best friend's wife; this poor, misguided soul attempted to snuff out his existence; luckily, he was unsuccessful. I could never comprehend why he didn't kick the piss out of Harry since he was more than capable of doing exactly that.

Harry was quoted in the local newspaper stating:

"No expense is spared when providing our students with nothing less than the best in terms of materials and technology in the classroom."

Of course, the media wasn't aware that the consumer math teacher was denied textbooks and spent the entire year running off copies of the teacher's text for his students.

By the way, the so-called threatening phone call turned out to be a complete misrepresentation, hyperbole at its worst; I phoned Vic later that night, following my arraignment in Sapp's office.

"Hello, Vic, it's coach."

"Coach W., it's great to hear your voice again. Are we going for pheasants again this year?"

"We're definitely going back to Red Butt to hunt; Vic, did you make a call to Giggalo last night?"

"Yes, why?"

"Well, Sapp called me into his office to inform me that H. Giggalo was irate because I requested the call; you woke his family, and your tone was threatening."

"Wow! I can see that things are only getting worse at that school, not better. Coach, you deserve respect, you've earned it. That poor excuse, what a hypocrite; he promises to help in any way he can, and, then, fabricates stories which cast us in a negative light. What's his problem anyway?"

"Vic, there's not enough time in the day to respond to that question; he's obviously trying to undermine our credibility and to frustrate our efforts to solidify the program. I would guess that he and Sam Stats are brainstorming in the wee-hours of the morning to devise some sinister, counter productive strategies.

"What's with Stats, too; if it weren't for wrestling, I would never have learned how to properly shed blockers or made All-State status in football. Coach, I'll personally call Sapp to tell him precisely what happened. You take care."

"Don't lose any sleep over this, Vic. Everyone knows what an idiot Giggalo is; I wanted to believe his motives were sincere, give him the benefit of the doubt, but he's just not trustworthy. Keep in touch, thanks for your help, bye."

Idiot or not, from this point forward, so long as there were ten or more former wrestlers in attendance at the public meetings or wrestlers' parents, the matter of the practice facility and the feeder program was "tabled" for further discussion. Of course, as I write the intermediate school has long been constructed, minus the wrestling room. We, still to this day, are forced to practice in the high school cafeteria, and the attempts at initiating the feeder have all been frustrated. Stats and his cronies are definitely responsible for our problems/ frustrations to date.

One final note; Giggalo is at it again; he was recently discovered in the newly constructed weight room in the act of consummating his baser sexual instincts with a newly acquired paramour by one of the custodians, who happened to be in the process of turning on the lights in order to dust the gym floor. Let there be light! He's being pressured to resign his position on the school board or be publically humiliated.

He doesn't deserve the option—a teacher in his predicament would be terminated and "blackballed" regarding future employment... but, then again, Harry is special simply because he's politically connected.

Chapter 26:

"The Legend Revisited"

Let's take time out in order to assess 'The Legend', Sam Stats, fabled football coach at Politico High School. None of us are perfect, but I want you to know that the following anecdotes are absolutely factual and are based on personal experiences.

My son started for the varsity football team his sophomore through senior year and he was offered "grants" or scholarships by every college and university he visited, including the Naval Academy. He also received the necessary Congressional appointment; however, immediately following the conclusion of the District playoffs and approximately a month and a half before his acceptance, the 'Legend' deposited all of Ross's paper work on another guidance counselor. To reiterate, Stats was also one of the counselors who did the very minimal in facilitating the students' transition from high school to college. He counseled much like he coached— old school through fear and negativity. He wouldn't present the kids with viable options so that they could make informed decisions; he discouraged many by telling them that they wouldn't be capable of completing college level work and that their money would be better spent on learning a trade or joining the military.

"Smith, why are you applying to that school; you couldn't handle the academics there; you lack the brains necessary to be successful there."

"There's just too much paperwork here for the Naval Academy, Laura; you take care of this, we have a big game coming up this week and I don't have the time, besides, I'm finished with him after this game anyway. The season is history and he's a senior."

This guy, much like Perfecto, loved hearing all of his crony supporters telling him what a wonderful coach he was and he took full credit; when the team lost, however, it was always the kids fault— they were stupid or he just didn't have the athletes. They weren't skilled or they didn't execute; his delay of game penalties in key situations or poor play calling had nothing to do with the losses.

"These kids' collective I.Q. is less than 100."

Stats never considered a kid's well-being/welfare and, as a result, many boys played hurt or aggravated an injury that could've been rehabbed with rest and exercise; the latter scenario often resulted in season ending, serious injuries.

"What are you, Ryan, a coward; you have a slight separation- big deal! Sometimes you have to play in pain for the good of the team."

Stats once started a boy at quarterback who fractured an ankle in the State playoffs, Not only did he start, but, he was called on to run the ball six times during the game. On first and goal inside the five yard line, he fumbled and P.H.S. eventually lost the game 14-13— how was that justified or fair to the other 29 members on that team? There were three other players who could have played the position and who would have improved the team's chances of winning and advancing in the playoffs. That was an unforgivable travesty.

On another occasion, a boy played the entire season after breaking his fibula; on the final play of the regular season, he re-injured the leg, fracturing it in the same place and, thus, complicating the situation by sustaining an additional hairline fracture. Stats' solution— don't play both ways (linebacker/center) just concentrate your efforts at center.

"Jeff, we really need you at center to execute our blocking schemes; you have to come through for us to win. You have to play or we don't have a prayer."

"Dan, your neck isn't going to be a problem this week, is it? You do realize that there are times when you have to suck-it-up and make sacrifices for the team. We'll fit you with a special horse collar or a harness. What do you say, big guy?"

"Coach, my entire left arm is numb and I don't have the full range of motion when I turn my head from shoulder to shoulder."

"It's probably just a 'stinger' or a bad bruise, nothing to really worry about. You'll be fine."

Well, it turned out that Dan wasn't fine. When wrestling season began, we made Dan go for a comprehensive evaluations; the doctors determined based on the MRI that he had experienced serious trauma, which caused damage to a small bone in his upper vertebra. They also stipulated that with the proper therapy and rest, they might be able to correct the problem. Dan never went for an evaluation during the football season because he feared losing his starting job.

At the banquet, Stats blamed his injury on wrestling, not

football; Dan pointed out that the problem originated during a blocking drill, which was supposed to measure one's manhood— shed three blockers and make the tackle. That year, two other players blew out their ACL's during the same drill...

These examples are just the tip of the iceberg. The 'Legend' was really a man's man... as noted previously, Stats constantly discouraged kids from bettering themselves, by competing in other sports. He demanded that they be under his tyrannical control 24-7.

When attempting to function as a guidance counselor, the 'Legend' miscalculated the GPA of a physically gifted prop 48 student, who was being recruited by several Division 1-A basketball programs, highly recruited. Fortunately, coach Lossi recalculated the points correctly and the student was accepted, started as a sophomore and eventually earned his degree from Penn State University with a 2.6 GPA.

Stats' response: "Lance will never play or graduate from that university; he's biting off more than he can chew. He'd have a better shot at a Division III school."

Stats, was also inclined toward displaying symptoms of paranoia, envy, and professional jealousy, not unlike the other members of the "Golden Boys". The District had received a state grant earmarked for refurbishing the football complex, and the Board decided that a tribute honoring former coaches was undertaken; Stats would be one of the honorees; unfortunately, he felt that his achievements surpassed the others contributions combined. He, therefore, demanded that his 'bust' not be included with the others since his legacy to the school and community were much more significant in his estimation.

Sam was also a deeply resentful person; as noted earlier, if another coach had a successful season and was fortunate enough to receive some positive press from the local media, he would downgrade or ridicule the sport or coach, always behind the coach's back. If confronted by the coach, Stats would plead ignorance or innocence regarding the matter. He was extremely envious of two other local coaches because they ranked ahead of him in wins, and it would remain this way for the duration of his tenure— he couldn't catch them. He constantly accused their programs of recruiting improprieties and unethical practices; he lived in constant fear that someone was always attempting to usurp his position.

I can't explain how or why, but this guy had amassed some serious political backing; bottom line, however would lead one to believe that he fancied himself a brilliant strategist and a consummate politician, first and foremost. He loved to play the role by rubbing elbows with the so-called "upper crust"— the man was and remains to this day, superficial as well as shallow, characteristics that he deemed to be his attributes, no doubt.

Chapter 27:

"A Final Insight"

Coach Tussi and I broke up a fight in the hall which took place during class time; following an investigation, these facts unfolded; the altercation was initiated by Shaun Murphy, the starting fullback, who threw the first blow. According to the school's discipline code, both boys should have been suspended for three to ten days, depending on the severity at the discretion of the principal. By the way, Murphy got his clock cleaned. The other student received the three-day suspension, while Shaun started at fullback the following evening; no reprisals were ever enforced.

When wrestling season rolled around, our 112 pounder was "nipped" for leaving the building without permission; he ran to the parking lot to get his cafeteria ticket. He was written up and suspended, a suspension, which would include missing Districts, and, therefore, Regionals and States. Talk about the punishment exceeding the crime! It was a most sinister act. How's that for a double standard. Ray would have been seeded first in his weight class...

"Napoleon" and all of his subordinates always got the benefit of the doubt, no matter what the infraction— let's hear it for <u>Animal Farm</u> and totalitarian societies; George Orwell would have never survived a day at Politico High School.

Chapter 28:
"The Merchant Of Venom"

When the new superintendent was selected, many of the faculty members became deeply concerned; once again, there were candidates who were more experienced and better qualified, but Dick Perfecto got the five votes necessary to secure the position of head administrator. What's the law—everyone will eventually rise to his own level of incompetence (case in point). Additionally, the guy was infamous with respect to his vindictive, backstabbing nature. He never had a kind word to say about anybody and he was unfounded as well as overbearing in his criticisms.

One of our faculty members, a dedicated and morally sound individual, attempted to take his life. Evidently, he was depressed and distraught by a number of issues, mostly familial related; after receiving therapy and rehab, Bert returned to work; he appeared to be a changed man. Perfecto commented matter of factly:

"Too bad Bert didn't follow through on his failed attempt because the guy has turned into a head case; he's nothing but a liability to everyone around him as well as to himself. What a total pain in the ass he's become."

"Dick your empathy and concern are really commendable.

You were his assistant coach for how many years? You guys shared in District championships; I thought you were close friends before you became assistant-principal. How can you be so calloused?"

"It's easy for you to say; you don't have to listen to his bullshit everyday. Fuck him! He should do everybody a favor and retire; he's useless.

What compassion, I thought...

"Dick, did you ever consider the loyalty involved in friendship?"

"I have no time for loyalty or friendship; he's too far gone."

Even when Perfecto functioned as a so-called teacher, he acted with impunity and arrogance, in that, the rules governing the rest of the faculty didn't apply to him; he was "above" we peons in the food chain, like some foreign dignitary who assumed political immunity. Dick taught like this—

"Do exercises A through F on pages 69-74", and off he went on his magical mystery tour to the teacher's room where he would socialize or talk on the phone with the local sports editor about his prowess as a coach. He also held conferences (X's and O's) with his basketball players outside his classroom while ignoring his teaching responsibilities; he was such a hypocrite in every facet of his empty life that he made me nauseous. He reveled in criticizing other faculty members "who didn't know the first thing about teaching", and Dick seemed to relish "bullying" the female teachers in particular.

In our district it seemed that the most conscientious, diligent teachers were repeatedly hassled, whereas, those who were inept or derelict in their duties were commended; quite a few of them, like Perfecto, became administrators who would then be entrusted to evaluate and rate the entire faculty— a Catch 22 at its worst! A few of them had no clue regarding whether a teacher was good or bad since they were such miserable failures themselves. Add to this scenario the possibility of a personality conflict and I think you can begin to get the idea.

During the 2000 wrestling season, we were fortunate enough to advance five boys to regionals and, finally, two to the State Championships; Jim Johnson placed third, while Kyle Smith finished fifth. When Perfecto was the assistant princi-pal, these two young men gave him some grief. Their home life was absolutely hellacious since their parents had alcohol/drug dependencies. Eventually, the booze and drugs snuffed out Mr. Johnson's suffering. Unlike Perfecto, I felt that they were really exceptional kids who required a little empathy and guidance. Following their success at States, the School Board debated whether or not they should be accepted onto the school's "Wall of Fame". Four weeks prior to this, the week before Districts, Perfecto made the following statement to me in the presence of fellow teachers:

"Personally, I don't give a damn how well they do or how far they advance; they're both fucking little scumbags as far as I'm concerned, and they'll **never** go on the wall or get any special recognition as long as I'm running the show here."

"Dick, Jim made the honor roll the last two semesters and Kyle's turning his life around as well; his grades have improved substantially and his attitude is very positive now. What they need is a pat on the back and some verbal encouragement."

"Hell will freeze over before that will happen, Art. They're bad news and that's that."

Well, it just so happened that the School Board seemed to share my sentiments, and they invited Jim and Kyle to the public meeting. I was also extended an invitation. Jim had to work and wasn't able to attend. Toward the conclusion of the meeting, we were asked to say a few words regarding our experiences at States. Kyle was both humble and surprisingly eloquent; throughout the season he and Jim had brought nothing but honor and positive press to Politico H.S. When Jim made it to the semi-finals and won his 100th victory, 11,000 fans gave him a standing ovation for his aggressive 18-3 decision. This reaction moved Jim to tears because both he and Kyle were constantly "booed" by fans since they were so dominant in league competition.

The other wrestlers on the team selected them co-captains; they proved to be, beyond any doubt, the very best leaders we ever had, and we were fortunate enough to have coached many great ones over a thirty year span. Their work ethic was truly remarkable; they always lead by example; they motivated their teammates with a poignant word or a kick in the butt, whenever necessary.

To place at States, one had to finish either 1, 2, or 3 at Districts and Regionals in order to advance; Jim and Kyle never wrestled before their freshman year and; yet, competed against District IV (perennial power) wrestlers at Regionals and States on their amazing trek to All-State status in their senior year. I doubt very much that this feat will ever be repeated in the state...

(Back to the meeting) When I was given the opportunity to speak, I implored the Board to set a precedent from that day forward—any athlete, no matter the sport, should be honored on the wall if he/she placed at States. Fortunately, Perfecto kept his mouth shut and they consented with 100% agreement. Of course, I also mentioned the practice facility and the junior high program for the umpteenth time. For me, the glass was always half full…

The latter turn of events ignited the ire and wrath of Perfecto who commented on the following day:

"Art, this won't be overlooked or taken lightly; you made me look bad last night before the Board and public, and I won't forget this indiscretion. You knew my feelings about those pricks and you're risking a lot at your own expense."

"Dick, you made yourself look bad. They're good kids who deserve a break in their lives, not another kick in the balls. Get over what happened two years ago and stop living in the past. Forgive and forget."

"Be forewarned, Art, and watch your back."

"Dick, are your threats physical or merely verbal in nature; I really can't believe that it's the former because nothing would be more appealing to me if that were the case."

"Art, we've been friendly for a long period of time, but this situation won't be tolerated; they're warnings that carry some weight and you should heed them if you value your job here."

"If you were in my position, you would have done the same to benefit one of your kids when you coached."

"Do you realize the cost factor involved here?"

"What cost factor, Dick?"

"Each frame alone will cost $160 and change."

"You're not paying for it with your own money, are you?"

"That's not the point; what if former students who placed come out of the woodwork and demand similar recognition?"

"If they placed at States, brought honor and notoriety to the school, then they belong up there; they should be so honored, as well. Nothing against football, Dick, but you've got 1st and 3rd team All-Staters on that wall who were known steroid abusers. Where's the merit in that?"

Chapter 29:

"To Hell and Back"

The events, which transpired at that School Board session fashioned and created a personal hell, and a sequence of events that would try and challenge, not only my professionalism but my faith/inner-spirit, also. Perfecto conspired with various individuals, including the new principal (hand chosen by Perfecto), in order to taint/question my dedication and character; Perfecto's vindictive dark side became apparent through his manipulation of others.

The plan that he set into motion went something like this; since the new principal was hand picked, Perfecto evidently instructed him to harass me and to make my life as miserable as possible at every turn. I tried to avoid the guy, but he would actually stalk me; from the get-go, it was easy to determine that he was sorely lacking in character; he lacked courage, exhibited defensiveness and immaturity, and was completely subservient to Perfecto's every whim. Following his first month on the job, if you were to poll the faculty, you would discover that Daniel Blank also lacked any degree of credibility or respect among the teachers. Any act, no matter how lowly, Dan would perform gladly for his puppeteer; this absolute became implicit to all in the kingdom. These guys considered themselves flawless in decision-making, in-fallible in judgment; they were incapable of even uttering these words: "Oh, you may have been right about that, I'm very sorry, my fault."

I'm a fairly quiet guy who listens more than he speaks; and, based on the conversations, which occurred in the teach-er's room, nary one teacher had anything of a complimentary nature to voice about Mr. Blank. The consensus of opinion in-dicated Dan to be insecure, arrogant and extremely unprofes-sional, and this is the hand I was dealt.

Over the span of thirty-two years and many different ad-ministrative changes, I always received positive, complimen-tary ratings; however, this clown maintained that my teaching lacked intensity and passion. This became the recurring theme over the next two years, no matter what I attempted to do with my students during his tedious, lame observations. The kids wrote and performed skits, there were listening dia-logues and exercises in the text; assigned library projects all in French. Despite the fact that it was only a second level class, I tried to create variety as well as challenge in order to have some fun and to avoid too much boring grammar. According to Dan, I had fallen short of my intended goal. Here's some-one who taught geography to junior high kids for five years and who possessed no knowledge of French whatsoever, and he's evaluating me—-what's wrong with this picture? Within the language department, if there were any questions regard-ing grammar, they were always directed to me. I wrote letters for the cafeteria's food service manager and for the elemen-tary guidance counselor, which were sent home to French-speaking parents. When I taught advanced classes, my better students won contests for writing and presenting plays, or for written exams that were administered by local colleges. But, I "lacked intensity and passion." Blank had become Perfecto's instrument of revenge...

Chapter 30:

"The Cat Fight"

One day, prior to homeroom, a fight erupted between two girls, neither of whom belonged in my room. I was returning from running off tests and getting a coffee. Immediately, I stepped between them (divide and conquer); evidently, the larger girl had gotten in a good punch outside in the parking lot. The smaller young lady appeared to have sustained a welt on her left cheek. I dispersed the gathering 'vultures', took names, and discovered that the dispute involved a boy, what a surprise! I had the injured girl, accompanied by a friend, go to the school nurse. The other one was sent to her homeroom so that she wouldn't be marked absent. I, then, filled out a student referral, complete with names, time, causes etc…and sent it to the assistant principal, Mr. Walton, who was in charge of discipline. Unfortunately, as my luck would have it, Walton wasn't in his office at the time and the referral got deposited on the receptionist's desk. I phoned the office and instructed Mrs. Hodge to page Mr. Walton and to give him the report before more trouble ensued. Somehow Blank got involved and took the matter into his own incapable hands. Following first period class, I was called and told to report directly to him. I thought, finally, Danny boy is going to thank me for a job well done—wrong again…

"Mr. Whiteknight, I've interviewed several students who witnessed the fight, and they all stated that you did nothing to break it up. What do you have to say for yourself?"

"For starters, Mr. Blank, I can secure at least ten students whose testimony will refute that of your witnesses. I resent your tone/attitude. Everything was detailed on the referral I sent to Mr. Walton."

"What referral?"

"Mrs. Hodge was the last person in possession of the referral because Tom wasn't in his office."

"Well, I wasn't aware of that."

"Well, perhaps when you've finished interviewing students regarding what did or didn't occur, you can find the time to read over the misplaced referral."

I walked out of his office and tried to maintain my cool and curb my temper; these were the scenarios with which I had to deal with on a weekly, sometimes daily basis. Dan, Mr. Professional extraordinaire, apologized to Mrs. hodge but he never said a word to me. A plethora of similarly negative confrontations would follow.

Chapter 31:
"Et Tu Brute"

The most aggrievous act, by far, was perpetrated during my last year of teaching; this experience was also instrumental in my determination to retire. It was the last day of classes prior to spring break, a Wednesday, and my double hernia was causing a considerable amount of discomfort; I informed the office at 10:05 AM that I'd appreciate being granted permission to leave before my last period class. I had already taught three out of four classes and had missed only one day that year. Fourteen of twenty-six students were absent and traveling with the band in Orlando, and they would have enough time to find someone to replace me. I had already spoken to several teachers who were willing to relieve me. Blank nor his secretary ever returned my call, so I made the necessary arrangements with the office. When the last class rolled around, I was really hurting. A couple of minutes into class, Ed Kelly showed up to cover the class, so I departed in good conscience. When I arrived home, I ingested a prescribed vicodine and laid down, hoping that the pain would dissipate. Susan (my significant other) and I were supposed to go on vacation to Myrtle Beach, but we couldn't leave until after 6 PM due to my physical problem.

Dick and Dan distorted everything; someone told them about my planned trip. This was all the information they required in order to contrive and fabricate their "frame-job". According to Ed, no sooner had I left my class when Blank appeared with his little clipboard to observe my class again. He had already performed this task that semester and it was Mr. Walton's turn in the rotation to observe me. They proceeded to contrive the following rendition regarding the sequence of events that actually took place.

According to their version, I **never** reported anything to the office (Blank's secretary would validate), and I left my class unattended; my physical ailment didn't exist; and, I had planned the whole incident to make my genuine intentions, the vacation to Carolina.

Certain members of the Board confided in me that Perfecto was attempting to garner five votes in order to get me "fired"; my pension would also be surrendered/lost after thirty-four years of service. The low-life failed to realize his goal; however, there would be some kind of disciplinary action taken in compromise. He had no clue that the Board members had spilled the beans, that they had confided in me because my word obviously had more credibility than his.

We met in the conference room where my fate would be determined; I was accompanied by the president of the teacher's union (Helen Jones) who pleaded with me to not do anything rash or out of character; we were long time friends. Just the expressions on their mugs made my skin crawl; I felt the urge to go primitive and clean house or to regurgitate on them in order to achieve some sort of Zen or a final catharsis.

The dialog began:

"Mr. Whiteknight, you're facing some serious charges here. What do you have to say for yourself? Things will probably go easier for you if you're honest with us. (**Honesty— neither of them was capable of defining the word.**) For example, this past weekend someone came forward who committed considerable damage to school property, and we decided not to prosecute since they were forthcoming and agreed to pay for the damages. Do you get my meaning?"

There he sat, Jabba-the-Hut, that pompous ass, that poor excuse, that shallow, empty husk of a person who fancied himself in control of my life. I had planned to play along until I had the opportunity to speak with the union counsel. I responded to Perfecto with my version (the truth). Their reactions became increasingly nauseous as Dick attempted to project himself as my friend and savior with more lies.

"You haven't been yourself lately, Art, and a lot of people have expressed concern with your well-being, including Mr. Blank and myself. We've been friends for quite some time now and I've noticed differences in your demeanor and attitude, also. Bottom line, whatever the problem might be, the Board is forcing my hand to delegate some type of action, short of termination of employment which, as you know, would result in the loss of your pension."

"Would you like me to attempt suicide, like Bert, Dick? Let's get this farce over with; do what you've been intending to do all along."

"Sorry you feel that way, but I'm going to have to suspend you without pay for three days; you can start today or on Monday, your choice."

"Gee, what a humanitarian; how ironic that I actually have

a choice in something. I anticipated the possibility of being be-headed or burned at the stake."

"Art, let's be civil and maintain our professionalism here."

"Excuse me, Dan, but I believe that I was addressing Dick, not you. Look (I leaned forward as if to stand, maintaining piercing eye contact directed at Perfecto while ignoring Blank completely) we all know exactly what's going on here and it stinks to the high heavens; this is, not only unjust, but totally repulsive as well. I'll start my sentence today and many thanks to you, Dick, for your kindness and honesty throughout this ordeal. Tell me something, how do you two characters man-age to sleep well at night; is it some mutation in your genetic make-ups or what?"

They lowered their heads in unison and did not respond…

(Outside the conference room) "Helen, did you see their lying faces? When I leaned forward, what did you sense?"

"Obviously, what I thought at that moment, that you were fixing to clean house with both of them. Blank was be-side himself because you chose to ignore him throughout the proceedings. Art, you're a great person / teacher and they're definitely not worth it; don't lower yourself to their depths; you're too smart for that. You had them wetting in their pants and it was quite entertaining. It's been an interesting day, take care of yourself and I'll let you know about the meeting with Jason Long."

" 'You reap what you sow', remember that. They'll have to answer someday for their dirty deeds."

"God willing, that's true but those two hypocrites are go-ing to burn in hell; on second thought, they may encounter difficulty making it there. They need to be put in their place;

pounding them into oblivion would not only be therapeutic, but it would definitely be a benefit to society. Do you want your children to grow up to be like those two jokers? The reason the world is in dire straits is because of lying bastards like them."

These "people" represented their personification of weak and spiritually empty human beings, devoid of character, lacking any saving grace. They embodied all that was sick and tainted in the world. Unfortunately, they were entrusted and empowered with the responsibility of administering the educational process; abuse of this authority was proving to be a very dangerous proposition for everyone involved.

Later that day, I met with counselor Long. He stated that I was within my rights to file a grievance but that I should be aware of a precedent which had been set in a similar case, whereby the teacher lost his job as well as his pension.

"There's a possibility you **could** lose, it's not really worth the risk. Art, count your loses and live to fight another day. Even the secretary seems willing to risk perjury over losing her job. If you had filled out a sick report in the office stating that you were ill, date and sign the damn thing; we wouldn't find ourselves in this situation. It's a shame that it's come to this, but this is the hand we've been dealt. I'm very sorry, Art, but that's the best advice I can offer at this juncture."

Chapter 32;
"A Final Decision"

There was an early retirement incentive in the contract and after thirty-four years of service, I decided that the stress and aggravation weren't worth it any longer; I would retire. Six months before my final teaching day, there was a final confrontation. Blank visited my classroom for his final evaluation, and when I received the rating sheet, he once again suggested that I should inject more intensity/variety into my presentation.

"I still haven't seen you at your best, Art; do you want me to come back when you're doing something special?"

I signed the rating sheet, which was satisfactory and tossed it across his desk.

"Listen, Blank, we are both very much aware regarding what you and your boss man pulled in attempting to frame me; we also know what prompted this whole, ugly mess. I want you to consider a sobering fact; certain people on the Board respect me; they informed me about Perfecto's futile attempt to get me "canned". He's certainly not a trustworthy person, nor is he a good friend by any stretch of the imagination. If I were in your position, I'd watch my back. What you've done is a travesty, unethical and unforgivable."

"Art, don't say something that you're going to regret later."

"What I regret is not challenging you two through the grievance process; I'm confident that I would have exposed you power-trip mongers, eventually. Remember one thing, Dan, you two couldn't muster the five votes necessary. What does that imply about your power and credibility?"

"Well, why don't you just let it go. Life is too short."

"This is far from resolved in my humble opinion; I have no intentions of forgiving or forgetting." (I figured that would create a little anx.)

"I must remind you, Art, there are still six months remaining in the year."

"Mr. Blank, you may take this any way you choose; your threats are empty and baseless; I'd strongly advise you to stay out of my immediate air space for the remainder of those six months. I still have options that I can initiate/pursue. Your main problem, and you possess many, is that you lack courage and balls-you're not a standup individual, you are seriously lacking in character in every respect."

I also shared these sentiments with Perfecto when the situation presented itself, after he approached me regarding my retirement plans. He wanted to wish me the best; we would always be friends; no hard feelings, etc... I suggested that it would be prudent on his part to call of his pitbull and to maintain a respectful distance. The clod was completely vacant of any degree of morality, it was sickening. And people question why public education is in such a sorry state...

Chapter 33:

"Super Indiscretions"

Two weeks passed and rumors began to surface implicating Perfecto's involvement in some shady dealings with respect to the four million dollar busing contract. The system continued to perpetuate decadence and corruption; remember, the original Board's members were all federally indicted and found to be as guilty as sin. They, each and every one, plea-bargained because they lacked the necessary "sophistication" in becoming consummate 'white collar' criminals who are usually adept at covering their tracks.

The young man I mentioned earlier, Jim Johnson, requested that I stand in for his mom on Parents Night for the senior football players since she would be out of town. I told him that I'd be honored; I was "touched" by his expression of respect. Many people commented about how moving and special that moment proved to be. The cheerleaders escorted us from opposite directions; we shook hands, hugged, kissed each other on the cheek, and verbalized our feelings for each other. There was a huge ovation throughout the stadium; it's an experience that will always remain with me.

On Monday, Perfecto ridiculed my participation in the Parents Night festivities by stating:

"Well, Art, I guess you have another mouth to feed; people are beginning to wonder if you're dating his mom."

Once again, an insight to his blatant, lack of character. Dick loved to find himself amusing; he couldn't relate to sensitivity, even if his life weighed in the balance.

Our fearless leader supposedly chose to emulate Harry Giggalo by carrying on an extermarital affair with some seriously desperate female; his son, who was actually a great kid, was arrested on several occasions for drinking-related incidents; and, Perfecto himself, fell victim to a vascular illness that required surgery. "You reap what you sow." Dick felt hatred toward me for whatever the reason, while I countered with sympathy/empathy for his misfortunes. Of course, I possess a conscience and a burning respect for my fellow man; whereas, Dick considered himself "above the law", free to do whatever he deemed to be politically expedient in order to realize his distorted sense of revenge or justice. Blank was nothing more than his pawn, someone to whom he'd delegate his dirty work; nonetheless, Dan loved his work and he "got off", euphorically high by fancying himself a "player", a person with power and influence over others who were subordinate to him, as he was to Perfecto. He couldn't relate to people. If Perfecto were ever present at the Lord's Last Supper, he would have been the first one out of the door with Judas to lead the conspiracy against Jesus for "cash on the nail".

What a sorry commentary— these guys had an awesome responsibility to the students and their parents, unfortunately, their priorities were askew; they simply couldn't see the forest through the trees. Expansion of one's power-base provided the only meaning in life and education's goal fulfilled.

Thank God that we are blessed with the volition to make choices, for I could no longer exist in that stagnant, regressive environment; I had grown weary of beating my head against the wall in an effort to affect a meaningful change. It wasn't complete frustration or a resignation to apathy; however, over the years, I know that my dedication and achievements made a difference to my students, athletes and peers. My accomplishments were noteworthy and a multitude of cherished memories were forever etched in my mind; memories, which were realized thanks to some very personal, meaningful experiences could **never** be trivialized or besmirched by anyone. Nominations by students who perceived you to be a solid teacher; selections by peers as the Region's Outstanding Coach in two sports; letters from former students thanking you for your inspiration in their lives; athletes who wanted to pattern their lives and careers after you; athletes and students who verbally expressed their gratitude and love; that's special…that's what matters most.

Chapter 34:
"Search For Meaning"

I've learned that in life it's not really fair to generalize or stereotype people because of many variables/complexities involved regarding the human character, but individuals like these seem to occupy positions of authority and control at an alarmingly increasing rate. The micro-institution of education is sorely in need of men of character and substance, not demagogues. Why are our young people falling further and further behind on comparative achievement tests?

Where are the Thomas Moores, the Quijotes who perceive the world as it could be, and not as it is? We are mourning the loss of heroes who people would strive to emulate.

In many respects the local school district has evolved to reflect and foster everything that's vacant and negative in society. "Cliques", I'm priority #1, the emphasis placed upon material possessions, drugs, teacher bashings; kids would rather have a car and work a job to pay for insurance as opposed to participating in a sport. Parents (including myself) are spoiling their children by trying to provide them with a better life than they experienced; the kids have learned to take things for granted and, consequently, expect more. I bought my first car (and every one since); I paid for my education while my sons did not. It's a strange, sociological phenomena, but perseverance and a strong work ethic are deteriorating among our young people.

The separation between church and state proved to be one of the most controversial issues confronting education; however, the main focus should have centered on banishing politics from the public school system. Politics festers with cronyism, nepotism, and hypocrisy; it's become an evasive cancer, which is consuming everything that represents goodness and morality. A person should be rewarded/advanced in the job based on experience, qualifications, and individual merit, not because he/she has "ties" to someone with political clout or connections. Character and intrinsic attributes have taken a back seat to a Machiavellian philosophy- "It's not what you know, it's all about who you know"- which has compromised the spiritual and sacred bond to our values. There's no justification for this, but, people like you and me who still give a damn must continue to fight the good fight; hope can be/is a powerful motivational force in our lives. There should be absolutely no tolerance for mediocrity or political compromise in education.

Chapter 35:

"The Ultimate Insult"

The year of my retirement, Andy Sanchez and I were fortunate enough to be selected League and Regional Coaches
of the Year, a significant and prestigious award because the
votes were cast by our fellow coaches who were polled by
the local sports media. This would be the third time that I'd
be honored while it was Andy's second; not too shabby for a
program which lacked so much. Hope sprang eternal and the
dedication/sacrifice of the kids certainly had a great impact
on the selection.

The League sponsored a banquet, which was held at the
conclusion of States where we placed three wrestlers: two
thirds and one at sixth; as a team we finished in the top ten.
Everyone involved in the program was thrilled. The restaurant, The Hemingway, was five-star quality and the anticipation looking forward to the presentation remained intense.
Our school usually had an excellent turn out since the top-
shelf food and drink were gratis; the previous year, a total of
fourteen people from P.H.S. were in attendance, however, this
year would be an exception. The administrators, the athletic
director, and all of their crony followers chose to "snub" us by
boycotting the annual celebration; hence the ultimate insult.

Every one of the other school districts was very well represented, however. Screwed over by the "Golden Boys" and their inner-circle of supporters, the only attendees included the coaches and the former athletic director.

One of our boys, Jim Johnson, was also selected as the Wrestler of the Year; when I approached the podium to accept the awards, I thanked my fellow coaches who deemed me worthy, our kids for their perseverance and spirit, Andy, of course, and our administrators for their refusal to attend. I received the expected response since everyone in the place seemed to empathize with our situation; we all had a good laugh at their expense. The majority of the coaches often expressed the sentiment that we deserved a lot of credit because they couldn't tolerate the crap or abuse that we had to endure.

The following day, as I expected, Blank once again became confrontational and accused me of making he and Perfecto appear as fools. Obviously, the write-up in the sports section with respect to my comments left them with a bitter taste and some emotional anxiety. But, hey, if the shoe fits, wear it.

"How can you sit there and point the finger at me, Mr. Blank? How can you justify or explain your blatant absence and your nasty insult? You're the guy who's always telling me that you don't hold a grudge."

"Mr. Whiteknight, I wasn't aware that you, Andy, and Jim were being honored or I would have been there; but that doesn't excuse your comments and behavior."

"Look, Dan, at least ten teachers on the faculty congratulated me yesterday prior to the banquet; besides, this past Sunday the Trib printed a feature story on my retirement and honor. Don't plead ignorance. What you guys pulled off last night by not attending was despicable and tasteless, and the comments I made were, most definitely, deserved. I made 'light' of an uncomfortable situation. Practically every person there was amused by my remarks and that was precisely my intent. We're the ones who were insulted and, therefore, we deserved the apology. Of course, I realize that we'll never get one; you and Mr. Perfecto can 'piss off' if you think that we are at fault."

For the first time in two years, Blank was at a loss for words; I stormed out and left him in his stupor. What a total jerk, a perfect ass-hole! Why did he think that he could intimidate me now after failing to accomplish that end for the past two years?

Andy, my "partner in crime" was a very unique person in many respects; he was blessed with a special ability to make people laugh; he never seemed to take life with all of its adversities too seriously. Luckily, he proved to be a loyal friend. Above all other considerations, he helped me maintain my sanity whenever the situation got tense; Andy opened my eyes to the fact that in the larger scope of life, what mattered most is how you treated your fellow man, what you've achieved in life, and the importance of your visions (dreams and goals). The meaning of one's existence, therefore, is fundamentally determined by/through one's contributions which should be directed toward a greater good.

There's a biblical allusion in Proverbs which prophesizes that: "Out of the **Sea of Politics** will arise the anti-Christ".... It doesn't take a rocket scientist to grasp the wisdom or intent implicit in that quote.

The Perfectos, Giggalos, and Stats of the world are not what they fancy themselves to be; in that, the "major players" who significantly influence our existence are usually men/women whose lives are focused on acts of humanity and humility. That's precisely why I chose to become a teacher. How can you find a better, more meaningful job where you actually have the opportunity to open kids' minds by broadening their horizons, touching their spirits, and motivating them to set goals and to dream, dreams? And, you get paid for this! I've received enough awards from my peers and letters from former students/athletes, which reinforces the hope that somewhere along the line, I have made a significant difference in their lives; and, for this I'll be eternally grateful.

On a personal level, this book represents my attempt to express priorities, concerns, and the hope that it may cast further insight into a serious issue confronting the educational process. On a daily basis, teachers are made more and more "accountable" for the multiple failures unfolding in public education. What about politically abusive administrators who lack integrity, morality, and vision? What about school board directors who are elected by the populace because they're socially prominent or politically connected; and, who are generally ignorant or misinformed concerning the key issues challenging education? Both should share/shoulder some degree of blame. Some of my earlier proposals might offer a viable solution, or, at least, a positive step forward. This spiritual journey was once a dream, but now it's evolved into a reality. Hopefully, for my kids sake and yours, things will change for the better...but, we must persevere in the task at hand; let's unite to take out the trash.

CPSIA information can be obtained at www.ICGtesting.com
Printed in the USA
BVOW02s2325050116

431886BV00003B/42/P